"Place all beverages on a flat surface, and swallow whatever you're eating or drinking before you begin reading...you're liable to lose it if you don't."

~**Ted Atoka** (author of *Fiammetta's Dream* book 2 of the 'Villa Paradiso' series)

"Many of you may have seen the fascinating musing of Robert Emmett... Believe me it's nothing compared to his quirky, amazing, bizarre, thoughtful stories."

~**Sherry Carroll** (author of *Even Rock and Roll Has Fairy Tales*)

"Robert is a natural... He has that ability to reach a reader's inherent flaws and expose them, because he is aware of his own. He is that artistic type, and having written music he understands the short burst of emotion, something the novelist needs to learn."

~**randall 'Jay' andrews** (author of *Inside the Circle*)

"PURR!"

~**Tessa B. Dick** (Raised by cats; author of *Philip K. Dick: Remembering Firebright)*

MEOWING ON THE ANSWERING MACHINE

ROBERT EMMETT

∞

Robert Emmett
Chicago, 2013

MEOWING ON THE ANSWERING MACHINE

A Selection of Short Fiction and Prose by Robert Emmett

Published by the author.
Manufactured in the United States and
distributed by **CreateSpace**.

All writings and drawings by Robert Emmett.

'The Writer Calls In Sick' written with P.T. Wyant.
ptwyant.com

Edited by Katie Ritcheske.

Cover Design by Kat Mellon.
kmwritingdesign.com

Photo by Sandra Schneiderman.

These stories were originally written between
1991 and 2013. This collection was compiled
and edited November 2013 thru January 2014.

The New Guise, Johnson & Grandparents, Unraveling and *Goat Wisdom* originally
published by Eat, Sleep, Write, October and
November 2013.
eatsleepwrite.net

Dangle, A Chicken Joint, Bleek, My Bodyguard, My Love, Taxiderm, World Intervention Week, Igloos, Coffee, American Idle, Sedna, Black Holes and *About the Author* originally appeared
in 'Igloos,' published by the author, 2004.

The Return of Couch! originally appeared in
'Postcards from the End of the World,' published
by the author, 1994.

FIRST EDITION, JANUARY 2014, PAPERBACK

irobert.me
robertwriting.wordpress.com

MEOWING ON THE ANSWERING MACHINE

A Selection of Short Fiction and Prose by Robert Emmett

1. The Writer Calls in Sick* 1
2. A Chicken Joint 4
3. Dangle 11
4. Johnson & Grandparents 13
5. Goat Wisdom 18
6. Coffee 20
7. The Long Game 23
8. The Comma Sutra 25
9. Bleek 29
10. My Bodyguard, My Love 31
11. Self Portrait with Nail 37
12. At War with the Spiders 42
13. Taxiderm 43
14. The Return of Couch! 50
15. Cat & Cockatiel 52
16. Black Holes 54
17. Unraveling 55
18. Sparks 58
19. Igloos 61
20. Tree House & The Gravid Moon 62
21. Streets Turned Ugly 70
22. World Intervention Week 71
23. The Lying Dog Sleeps 79
24. Unseen Architect 80
25. Drunk Dialing 84
26. Garage Door Revisited 85
27. Humans 88
28. Headlong 91
29. Abraham Presley 93
30. The Zipper 95
31. Cleansing 99
32. Subroutine 101
33. Yarn 103
34. American Idle 121
35. God's Writing Group 123
36. Jettison 126
37. The New Guise 129
38. Emmanuel & Zina 134
39. Destiny 135
40. Sedna 137
41. Fly 143
42. (invisibility) 145

About the Author 147

Afterthought 149

*'The Writer Calls In Sick' written with P.T Wyant

This one goes out to Anna,
from your Uncle Cookie...

THE WRITER CALLS IN SICK

by Robert Emmett and P.T. Wyant

Dear Editor,

I have bruised my finger and cannot type today. It hurts to bend the digit. It stretches the scar and causes it to crack across the surface. I bleed on the page. The words are smeared together in a shadow of red. Every word comes with pain. Every letter I tap out is a reminder of the injury I sustained.

> Dear Writer,
>
> Put a Band-Aid on it, take a Motrin, suck it up, and get to work.

Dear Editor,

I am taking your advice and trudging through. If my sentences start to run on and meander more than usual, it is probably only dizziness from blood loss. Also note the addition of a new character in the story, the evil-minded copy editor with little compassion and no friends at all, who meets a brutal but fitting demise. Be assured this is a fictional character, and any similarities to real people living or soon to be dead are purely coincidental.

> Dear Writer,
>
> The new character has been duly noted and will be dealt with when your manuscript finally crosses my desk. In the meantime, please be aware that I am working on a prequel to your novel. Its plot

revolves around a whiny, self-absorbed, wannabe writer who should give up as a novelist and instead write a book titled *Excused for Missing Deadlines...* and said writer's patient and long-suffering editor.

Dear editor (capitalization intentionally omitted),

Please forward a link to your new work to NASA scientists who are searching for proof of Black Holes. I look forward to the new volume and will add it to the list of other works I've never heard of and cannot find. I believe my local bookstore now has an 'Obscure and Forgotten' section where I may one day find your alleged writings.

Dear Writer,

Ah! So that explains where your books have been shelved. I was beginning to wonder...

Love always,

Your ever-patient editor

P.S. I am glad to see that your finger is feeling better. Now, about that manuscript?

Dear "editor,"

Finger is feeling much better, but I am now too pissed off to write. Expect four or five thousand words on the subject in your inbox in the morning.

Dear "writer,"

That's fine. Please anticipate a four-to-five-month delay in your advance.

Dear Militant Tyrant and Apparent Heir of Wisdom and the One True Way,

Fine! I will wrap my mangled digit so as not to frighten or offend the delicate sensibilities of some of the folks in the office. I will be in within the hour, if my presence today is absolutely essential. Had I known I would be working in such a rigid and stifling atmosphere, I would never have chosen to write children's birthday cards.

Should I pick up donuts on the way?

Yes, please. Preferably jelly-filled so that any stray blood does not frighten the secretaries. I'll put the coffee on – it's going to be a long night.

A CHICKEN JOINT

From the front, it looked like any other greasy spoon, the family-style restaurants slapped together wherever two roads meet. I was beckoned around the side of the building by the unmistakable smell of live animals and the clucking of a full chorus of chickens.

"Sir," the hostess called from the opened front door, "I can show you to your table now." She stood half-hanging out of the restaurant, propped against the doorjamb, peering at me expectantly. As far as she was concerned, this was going to be my only chance to eat in this lifetime; perhaps she was willing to make it her business.

She drummed a pen against a pad of paper, waiting for me. I stood at the edge of the building, wanting to see what was going on behind it. Stuck there in one of those moments where I couldn't tell which way I really wanted to go, I paused and balked as the hostess smacked her chewing gum in contempt. My curiosity gave way to hunger, as it always will, and I let her lead me in to where I could be fed.

"Do you keep real, live chickens here? Out back?" I asked. I slid down into the booth she had gestured me toward, pulling against the wall and away from the nasty woman.

"If you call them real," she muttered as she walked away.

"Hi! Welcome to SMC," a large man said to me immediately. He was overly fed and looking too happy to be doing his job. A smile too wide bobbed above a mass stuffed into a white dress shirt; the manager, I noted. "Is this your first time dining with us, sir?"

I started to ask him, "Do you really keep live–"

The door to the back of the restaurant slammed open, startling the room; a few gasps escaped from scattered customers; utensils smacked against glass. Even the old nasty hostess sitting at a back booth intently smoking cigarettes turned to see what the commotion was.

"Dad, I can't find the stapler," a teenage voice called out. I saw the boy's hand for only a second, and then there was a crash, plates and metal colliding, a muffled sound of clumsy steps and stifled expletives.

"My son," the large man announced, his fake smile sliding to a sincere joy. "I'm trying to teach him the business." He let out a long, resigned sigh and then yelled toward the back, "Darold, I was just using the stapler. It should be somewhere right around the desk."

"I looked by the desk!" the voice came back, enunciated with a groan at the end.

"*On* the desk; in the middle is my planner. To the left is the computer, and to the right is the phone. Right between them, at the top of the planner, is where I keep my pens and my tape and my punch and my stapler."

Another groan came from the back. "I'll look there. Again."

Once we were sure the ruckus was over, the large man turned toward me again, his fake smile already bright and intimidating. "Now, how can we help you this evening?"

"What did she mean when she said, 'If you call them real'?" I asked him, nodding toward the hostess, who was now glowering at me.

"Perhaps I should explain SMC technology," the man said. He wiped at his brow with the menu in his hand and began the arduous task of sliding himself into the booth, directly across from me.

"SMC?"

"Self-Microwaving Chicken," he announced in an excited whisper once he was situated; his eyes lit up upon uttering the words, and he licked his lips before continuing. "These guys have been genetically engineered with radioactive chemicals lying dormant in the coding of their DNA. Once a certain impulse synapse of the brain is switched on, the chicken's body quickly works to produce these elements, causing a small fission reaction and then cooking itself to a golden, juicy, crispy perfection."

He watched me for a reaction, but my mind wouldn't let me respond, seeming to be out of order until I could properly process what he had just told me.

"You see, it's a three-way switching mechanism. There are three ways to cause the production and release of–"

"I found the stapler," the teenage voice called again, muffled through the door. "It's broke, Dad. It won't staple."

His dad smiled apologetically at me. "Darold, you probably just have to put some staples in it."

"Where are the–"

"On my desk. With my tape and my pens and my punch."

He waited before looking at me again, staring at the door toward the back, hoping he had given the boy enough instruction to occupy himself for at least a little while.

"Where was I? Do you want to see one?" Without waiting for an answer, he swiveled his body around toward the hostess sitting in the back. "Hessa, can you go grab us a chicken?"

She glared at him from behind a cloud of cigarette smoke for a few tense seconds. As soon as she was moving, she was muttering under her breath, "Get me a chicken. I'll get you a frigga fracka chicken." It became impossible to understand her as she moved across the restaurant to a door leading out behind the small building. It pushed open with a creak.

"Hey, which one you bastards wants get et?" Hessa cackled at the chickens as she walked through the door and into their midst.

They scurried away at the sight of her, clucking and flapping. A few feathers caught wind and were carried into the restaurant through the open doorway.

After a minute, Hessa appeared again, the cigarette between her lips splitting a crazy smile; the chicken - held by the neck like a flashlight, bobbing and bouncing off her hip with each step - was very much alive but seemed resigned to her grip.

"Here's your chicken," she said as she plunked it down on its own two legs on top of our table. It just stood there, staring blankly ahead of itself, making no move to run. Hessa turned with a sort of half laugh. "Enjoy!"

"This!" The large man held his arms out on either side of the chicken, like it was a sacred offering. "You see, it looks like an ordinary chicken. Wings, beak, feet, tail. But look here." With his thumb and forefinger, he spread feathers away from the breast, revealing a dark, raised area in the skin. He gestured for me to look closer, and at first I thought it was almost like a cherry-red fingernail, perfectly round and translucent. Poking out of the surrounding skin, I saw a little red plastic button.

"That's how you cook it?" I asked.

"Just press the little red button and wait," he said, mocking a tapping motion to instruct me - but also there was an undeniable glint of hunger in his grin.

I started examining the chicken, moving feathers around and trying to coerce the animal to open its mouth. "Where are the other two triggers?"

"Ah, well, you see, it's not like that." The man shot me a little disappointed glance and pressed the button himself. It lit up red, and the chicken stood as if at attention and slowly began to rotate. "That is the second part of the triple-triggering device, when the chicken reaches full adulthood and is switched on to cook. The first part of the trigger would happen much earlier. If this chicken had never become a chicken, that egg would have released the nuclear elements into itself after a predetermined period of time, producing the best damn hard-boiled egg you've ever had."

My mouth started to water. Maybe it was the authoritative and passionate way this man before me talked about food, and maybe it was the slow-spinning chicken in front of me, the completely unnatural chemical reaction occurring within its skin already giving off a pleasant aroma. I licked my lips and gave him a quick, impressed nod.

He continued, "Now, the third part of the trigger–"

"Dad, where's that thing to make the holes in the paper?" The voice of the teenage boy jarred us from our peace as it shot from the back room.

The man sighed and rolled his eyes. "The three-hole punch," he yelled into the air. "It's on my desk where I keep the pens and the tape and the stapler."

The boy let a long groan roll out and stomped off.

I found myself momentarily hypnotized by the spinning chicken, standing perfectly still with its eyes shut, but rotating slowly, steadily in place. It looked to be in a deep trance. The feathers seemed to have turned to dust and drifted away, and the bare skin was beginning to glow a pulsating golden hue. My stomach churned against itself and growled.

"How do you know when it's done?" I asked.

"It will stop spinning and beep. Let it stand for two minutes before serving."

"Beep?"

"It will beep," he explained, "just like a microwave oven does. Beep- Beep- Beep- BEEEEEP. At first they had it 'cluck' when it was done, but a lot of people found that to be too morbid."

"Ask him what happens if you eat it before it's done," the hostess yelled to me, situated again at her booth in the back. She let out a nasty, evil cackle and nodded at me, taking great joy in our conversation.

"Dad!" The boy pushed the door open slightly, and I could just make out his face. He looked almost exactly like a younger, slightly smaller version of his father. "Where do you keep the extra holes? I can't get the three-hole puncher to punch. And I already looked on your desk."

A strange expression came over the man's face: part fear, part defeat, part confusion, and some things I couldn't quite place. "Darold, it's probably just jammed. Here – bring it here."

"It's the third trigger," Hessa yelled, still smiling insanely. She sucked on her cigarette and continued, a low fog of smoke spilling out over her lip. "If you go and eat that chicken before it's fully cooked, before all that nuclear stuff has done its thing, the radioactive chemicals get into you, get mixed up in your DNA. And then it gets passed on to your kids. Isn't that right, Darold?"

Now standing before his father, who was fidgeting with the punch, the boy gave Hessa a meek, silent look. She let a long, slow report of laughter ring throughout the restaurant, reverberating off the ceiling's wooden crossbeams and echoing against the windows.

I sat, quiet and tense. The hostess continued to giggle and now cough occasionally. The manager, completely absorbed, his face red and visibly wet, pulled bits of paper from the three-hole punch. Darold stood dumbly gawking, his acne-riddled face only half visible under his long, greasy locks of black hair. A small wheezing of breath was his only notable sign of life.

The chicken suddenly beeped, and I nearly leapt out of my seat. I laughed, realizing it was our food, and held my hand against my chest to still my racing heart. The man across from me was smiling again, his eyes alight in anticipation of tearing into the bird.

Even Darold now looked alive. He lifted his head a little to regard the chicken and licked his lips. He smiled and brushed his hair away from his face. I saw his father's intensity in his eyes, but I was taken aback by what looked like a huge pimple directly in the middle of his forehead. My heart dropped into my stomach as I realized, unmistakably, that it was a little red plastic button.

DANGLE

Have you ever noticed Architecture isn't really well-represented in tattoo art?

The reason I bring it up is personally I am alarmed and somewhat apprehensive about the apparent trends of tattoo art these days. I'm not talking about the avant-garde skin-graft conceptual sculptures they are webbing together with needle and ink in the basement parlors of France and Denmark. I am talking about the very real and very dangerous trend in body art known as Medical Mimicry.

It began with fake moles and scars but has escalated recently into grotesque representations of tumors and skin conditions, such as eczema and jaundice.

Do you remember Dangle? I know that's not his real name. Everyone called him Dangle, but that's another story for another time.

Do you remember he saved up his insurance-fraud money for six months and then went to get his leg done up to look like the latter stages of diabetic gangrene?

Do you remember that? He came home all drunk and spitting venom, saying he got ripped off. He pulled up his pant leg to show us the tat, and we were all disgusted and amazed. Dangle, though, insisted it didn't look authentic, it wasn't real enough.

And do you know what happened?

The other night we were at that seedy intellectual bar where Dangle likes to hang out, cowering together around a wobbly table and a few dark pints of mysterious-tasting poison. Dangle was buzzed and as usual started into his Frank Lloyd Wright diatribes, his whispered pleas rising to fevered crescendos about the 'Damned rules of Architecture'.

Apparently he caught a few ears with his rants and ended up arguing with a half dozen bikers. Real mean-looking guys, the type of guys who drink Jack Daniels on their Harleys whilst extolling the virtues of Mies van der Rohe. Needless to say, it got ugly pretty quick. In the ensuing melee, Dangle was knocked unconscious when a flying beer keg got in the way of his head. Police and paramedics were called to the bar, and Dangle was taken out on a stretcher.

He had a major concussion and, with the aid of medication, was unconscious for three days. When he finally awoke, the doctors said there was no permanent damage to his head and that he would fully recover in a short time. But, they said, there was another matter.

When he arrived at the hospital, it was quite a frantic night in the emergency room, and he was examined rather quickly. It wasn't until after they had amputated his left leg that the surgeon realized the gangrenous atrophy was merely a tattoo.

"You cut off my leg?" Dangle twisted his face into a curious pucker of disbelief. "You thought the tattoo was really decay?"

"Yes." The head of surgery humbly offered the amputated leg to Dangle so he could see for himself. "We are deeply and truly sorry, sir."

Dangle took his former limb and ran it around in his hands, like warming up a baseball bat, reexamining the extensive artwork stitched into the skin and admiring it now in a new light.

"Nice." A sly smile crept up one side of his mouth. He nodded in approval. "Very nice, indeed."

JOHNSON & GRANDPARENTS

It's tough to find a good time-travel provider these days, someone reliable as well as affordable.

The commercialization of the Time-Line brought the usual lazy capitalists into the arena, companies that built their fortune by billing for weight and the distance-in-years to the destination. All of known history was soon cluttered and muddled, and it is no longer possible to discern exactly when it started or how long this has been going on.

Some will say it was a mistake for Abraham Lincoln to make such wide and lasting declarations praising the temporal-transportation industry. Some of the older citizens among us still swear they remember a version of the Gettysburg Address without the discourse on time travel.

It's impossible to prove one way or the other. Anyone with the latest version of *LinearShop Pro* can go back and redraw the events for all of us to recall any way they choose.

It took a true pioneer, and a man reared and trained in the financial world, to see the true promise of this new enterprise. It took a man the caliber of Digg Johnson to see an exponentially greater vision for time travel and intuit what could happen when money was involved.

It is said his first transporter was nothing more than a plastic *Fisher Price Time Machine* play set, upgraded and reengineered with some nano-Lego technology. Rumor is Digg didn't build it at all; it was really his mostly silent, brooding cousin Chasm Johnson who put the contraption together. But Digg figured out how to use it correctly, how best to utilize this novelty of jumping through the years, slipping from present to past and future and back. He dreamed of interest rates collecting in non-Euclidean geometrical piles. He declared that the buck need never stop and could indeed inflate and expand as vast as the Universe around us.

When he first formed his company, *Johnson & Grandparents*, it was barely noticed. The Big Three had already built their reputations with clever monikers and flashy, sophisticated marketing campaigns. *The Clock Setters*, *Deja View* and *Calendar Arrangements* were household names, even then, for all your historical or future needs. The market has always been littered with upstarts and local individuals; there are a few legitimate business ventures designed to compete and an almost endless line of guys who built a trans-mat in their garage looking to turn a quick profit.

So initially the name *Johnson & Grandparents* made little if any impact. It sounded quaint, recalling family businesses often named for the owner and his sons. Few were impressed by the retro-sounding brand, and more got the wrong impression altogether, put off by the old-fashioned ideals it evoked.

But when the world realized what the name meant, and what Digg Johnson had actually achieved, history collectively paused for a momentary breath and tried to grasp the full potential of this new, forward-thinking business model.

Digg had really hired his grandparents to work for him, as the name implies. But he went back to the 1960s and picked their teenage selves out of time. Young, bright-eyed, strong and filled with questions and wonder, they showed up in the present day with a nostalgic work ethic. And that wasn't even the truly genius part of Digg Johnson's plan. He didn't simply pluck his grandparents from the past and plant them here. They were the first to commute.

You may remember that back then, Temporal Transportation still had a formal and distinguished feel. They say the same was true of early air travel: people used to put on their nicest suits before boarding a plane, and the whole affair was treated with reverence. Not like today where the runways are littered with rogue pilots and underground airlines, where thousands of freeloaders will chase any flight off the ground, trying to hop on the wing or fuselage, hoping to huddle together with dozens of other castaways who managed to make it atop the plane.

Time travel in those early days was such an expensive and energy-consuming event. Plans were made well in advance and were usually treated as nearly permanent shifts in the time stream because most people could never afford to do it twice.

Digg was the first to see the benefits of tunneling his ancestors from the '60s every morning and then shooting them back every night. And he always dropped them off just five minutes after he took them, in the morning while they were still getting ready for school. No one ever knew they were gone. Although it did mean his grandparents, Budgie and Tandy, were in effect experiencing 36-hour days. This is often cited as the theory, or at least part of it, behind why the elder Johnsons seem to age so much more quickly than the rest of us.

The real feat, though, was in how they invested their money. Digg Johnson paid his employees considerably well by today's standards, but when Budgie and Tandy returned home every evening to the land without computers or space explorations or even color television, they found themselves suddenly filthy, almost unimaginably, rich.

They had more money than they would ever be able to spend in one lifetime and ended up leaving a good fortune to their descendants. In one of his final interviews, Digg admitted this substantial inheritance was what allowed him to get his time-travel business off the ground in the first place.

And old Budgie and Tandy Johnson seem none the worse for wear. Many were suspicious early on, especially in the medical community, who were worried about the potential effects of repeated exposures to time shifts on the body. But the Johnsons are still able and alert, even if slightly more elderly than most folks in their early thirties.

They say Budgie has developed a little tic. He will be standing there having a conversation with you, when he will seem to dissipate into static, sort of disembodied and distant, a blurry image of his usually solid stance. But if you give him a slap on the side, a light tap like you'd give an old TV to steady its picture, Budgie pops back into focus and continues talking like nothing at all happened.

Digg, though, no one can say whatever became of Digg Johnson. Some say various legal wranglings were finally getting a grip on him and sent him into hiding. Others claim his massive fortune made him incredibly powerful but ever-increasingly paranoid and reclusive.

A few articles still exist, an interview here and there that he was purported to have granted. But there are no pictures, and no one still living can admit to ever having talked to him or even having seen him in real life. His signature on the corporate charter for Johnson & Grandparents and the audiotape of the speech he gave in the middle of the Comedy Central roast of Pope Light Bringer the Sixth are the only tangible links we have to this man who so changed the world and our memories of it.

Some claim he's a god of sorts, or whatever the 21st-century equivalent of a god might be. Others despise him and will spit at the mention of his name. For the most part they can't quite remember why and are lost to translate their hatred of the man into words. But they assure us it is an obscene and unthinkable injustice Digg Johnson has committed against us all.

And many agree that this is why he disappeared. So many blamed him for the sad, twisted state of the world, and some wanted revenge. But Digg Johnson, being ingeniously inventive as well as shamelessly opportunistic, had taken precautions to remove any evidence of himself and any proof of his involvement in any sort of endeavor. They say his wealth and power afforded him an unprecedented control over time, and in order to avert any guilt or blame, he had written himself out of the story completely.

GOAT WISDOM

The man came upon a clearing; it was just like his dream. He wiped a few droplets of sweat from his forehead. Trees stood around the perimeter, stretched high and leaning in, a mezzanine of green opening up to the sky.

It took him a moment to see the goat; this he had not expected. He approached the center of the clearing. The goat looked on, aware of the man but uninterested.

The two stood before one another. The man furrowed his brow a few times, squinting at the goat. His mouth opened and closed; a laugh and a scream fought for passage in his throat. Neither could get by.

The goat stared back, preoccupied by a slow, circular chewing motion. A few silent minutes were allowed to pass before the man finally spoke.

"Greetings, wise goat, as I must assume you to be. I have traveled far, led by a dream, to find this clearing so that I may attain ultimate wisdom."

The goat stared back, with no indication of understanding or even hearing the words; it continued its slow chewing motion.

"I have left my home and my family, my friends and society." The man let his voice become bolder. "I have come seeking knowledge, truths about this life and its meaning, answers to questions about what must come after."

The goat stared back and continued to chew.

"I ask and I beg that if you have these answers," the man continued, gaining volume as frustration crept into his words, "please give me a sign, a gesture, a clue! Wise goat, if you are, I must know where we come from before we are born, and where do we go when we die?"

The goat stared back, continued to chew.

The man's eye twitched with exhaustion. He felt his cheeks flush, and anger swept through him. "I ask you these things, and the reply is silence. I beg, and you simply look on." The man was nearly shouting now. "I'm afraid my dream has led me astray, for you are but a lowly goat and know nothing of meaning, of life's wisdom, or certainly of what comes after."

The goat stared back; its face was now still.

Wholly fed up with the man, the goat ate him.

COFFEE

So Juky and I are in that new coffee shop the other day, the one downtown where they charge by the syllable, *Tetra-Mocha-Ton*. Supposedly there is a seventy-two-syllable combination that - when deciphered by a trained *Caffeinologist* (the minimum-wage staff in the shop), mixed together properly in a brown paper cup, and then consumed by the purchaser - would put one in direct contact with the universal Supreme Being.

A lot of the people who have been flocking to this place since it opened maybe two weeks ago are really buying this story.

I don't. I think it's nothing more than a way to gouge the coffee-drinking crowd, especially the spiritually desperate among them. It reminded me of the rumor going around the theological technophile circles a few years back - someone had claimed to have stumbled upon God's personal email address, but being two hundred sixteen characters long, it was automatically refused by every known email provider.

It is my turn to order. I stand before the gray-uniformed kid who will take my order and convert it into liquid. I am scanning the menu, a single folded page detailing the complex key of coffees and ingredients and additives that are available and how to incorporate them into your drink.

I recognize the basic formulas of a sophisticated linguistic system. Each of the different types of beans, or whatever, that can be made into a drink forms a sort of root word, which is conjugated to denote different sizes and strengths. And then the word is built up with suffixes and prefix fragments denoting things such as 'two packets sugar, one packet Splenda, 1/2 tbsp goat milk, and one ice cube'.

The kid behind the counter is waiting for me, pencil in hand to jot down every utterance.

"Coffee," I say, and dare not utter another sound. He stares at me for a few tense moments, his pencil pressed against the pad.

Coffee. Two syllables, one dollar. Had I said 'large coffee', it would have been a dollar fifty, 'me-di-um co-ffee' would have cost me three. We learned the first day this place was open that anything uttered to your Caffeinologist when you had their attention would cost you, and even saying something such as 'just a coffee' would have doubled my price.

Juky is standing behind me, mumbling through a nonsensical string of sounds. He's looking for the grail, the Tetra-Mocha-Ton. But I can't tell what he's going to order; this place seems to have every variation of coffee drink available and an astonishing list of ways to make them and what to put in them, everything from amaretto to absinthe.

A few fragments of Juky's rambling become lucid in my mind. He's running through the possessive-tense variations of a banned sweetener, the one that was taken off the market just recently – the one they were testing as a drug to relieve motion sickness, but which caused agoraphobia in most of the test cases. Doctors can't even prescribe this stuff anymore, but this place can serve it – due to a slippery loophole in FDA guidelines – if it is ordered correctly in this cryptic caffeine-language.

The kid behind the counter hands me a hot brown paper cup, with a hot brown paper heat shield for my hand, and takes my dollar.

I turn to look for available seating and see that most of the people waiting in line are chanting in the odd cafelalia; some with tongues jutting from their mouths, some looking heavenward with eyes rolled into their heads. The entire shop is filled with a dull cacophony of nonsense. A few scattered patrons seem to roam around the perimeter of the tables in a trance.

Juky is silent for a moment as he steps up to the counter. He lowers his head and breathes, slow and deliberate. The kid behind the counter flips to a fresh sheet on his pad. He stands with pencil ready as Juky begins to bleat.

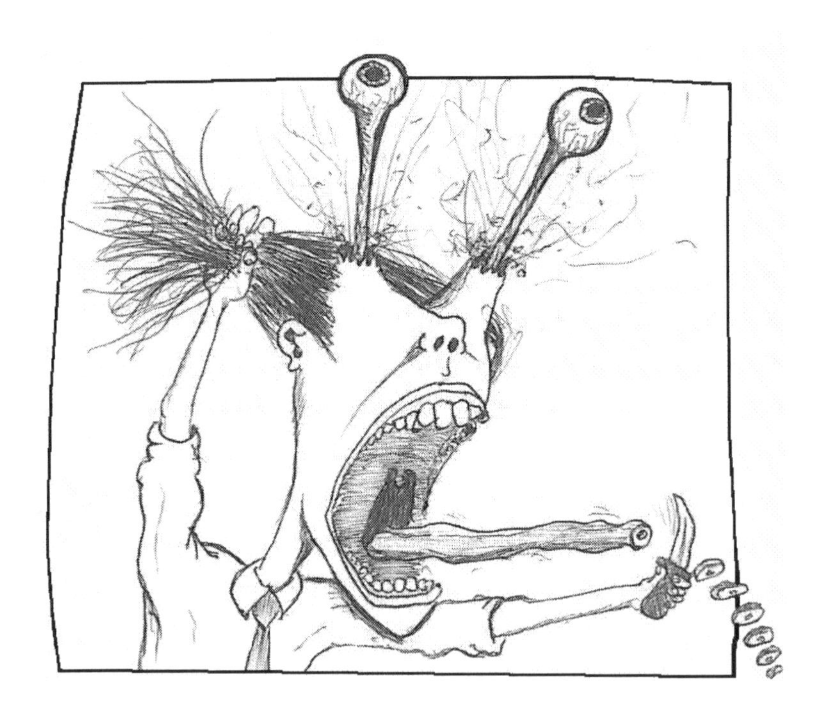

THE LONG GAME

They heard the chopper in the distance. If there had been any doubt, they saw it was unfounded and abandoned it at once. Blaid stood in front of the troops, standing tall now, confident.

The regularity of the attacks and their ability to cripple the community, a dark devastation in every generation, made many lose any hope or ambition. For a few, though, like Blaid, it worked to reinforce their resolve. The approaching clamor, the sound of the attackers' jarring, repetitive pounding, made him struggle to stand even taller, rigid and proud.

"The chopper is on the horizon," Blaid shouted for his company to hear, not looking away from the terrible machine that had rolled into view. "This is it, everyone. Stand firm and fight smart. You may be overwhelmed by the size of our enemy, for it is truly immense. But we are greater collectively. One of us wouldn't last a second in the enemy's grip, ripped in half with barely a thought or effort. But together we band and are bound. Many of us will not return from this battle, but together in our great numbers we will suffocate the beast who brings our sacrifice, bite the hand that feeds us our mortality."

Blaid swallowed hard as the shadow crawled over him. His heart sank. The chopper was even bigger than the old stories had described, and he'd always considered the children's fables to be exaggerated tall tales. But their message was true, and it was the same message as that of every song and story of his people: 'Once in every lifetime, when we grow as tall as we will grow, the enemy will come to cut us down.'

More frightened than he'd ever been, Blaid was unable to utter another word to his troops. His throat had tied itself into a hard, dry knot, and the sound of the enemy nearly on top of him would have rendered it impossible anyway.

The wind whipped against him harder than he'd ever imagined it could. He repeated his mantra and intent under his breath, determined to damage, a deep hunger spilling out from his every pore, that his tiny contribution may be measured in and add up one day to defeat the unknown enemy.

The giant was upon him now, the darkness complete, the clang and crash of the machine smashing against itself as it chewed and kept hunting. Blaid prayed and longed to be useful one final time before he was extinguished.

The motor stopped, and a loud thud shook the ground.

Myfanwy looked up from the paper. She took a sip of her coffee, stood up and went to the window, pulling the spongy blue curtain aside.

She saw her husband on the ground and shot out the back door.

She found him in the yard, next to the mower, both laid out on their side. A thick clump of fresh grass clogged the mower's blade. She knelt beside the man; a tear fell from her eye and splattered on his cheek, but he didn't react.

Myfanwy lifted her husband's head and studied his wide, staring eyes. His cheeks and throat were swollen. She pushed open his mouth with two delicate fingers. His green lips slithered apart, and wet clippings spilled out, down his chin.

She dug her hand in to scoop everything out. She pulled a few handfuls but saw no end. Somehow he had inhaled a lung full of fresh-cut lawn and had choked on a twisted knot of grass.

THE COMMA SUTRA

I thought it was a joke at first. A mild ribbing from a friend who said I used too many commas. I know I sometimes over-punctuate and have some funny ideas about marking the pauses and full stops. And I do lean heavily on the single closing curve that rests along the baseline.

Last night a few members of my writing group stopped by. They joined some of the more lucid and literate frothing Internauts I trade verbal slashes and stabbings with on Reddit and Facebook and in YouTube comments. They wanted to talk about my reliance on the comma. It was not a joke.

One at a time and without pause they spelled out what my sloppy punctuation had done to each of them. The time and frustration and medical expenses I had bestowed on them individually. Each comment was an ice pick at my frozen delusional shell.

I grew overwhelmed as the admission cemented inside me. The guilt overflowed and spilled out of me. I recalled my love for the seemingly insignificant small symbols we use to frame our words and instruct their meaning. I thought it was innocent when it began. Near the end of a rambling sentence that became a laundry list of complaints I jabbed three dots on the page after 'et cetera'. Three dots that could go on forever. I shivered. A static tingle tickled my skull.

I found the semicolon and the *em dash*. My habit shot up to four or five thousand words a day. The more ellipses and umlauts and squiggles and ephemera in my employ the longer my frayed strands of logic could be tied together going well past the physical comfort zone before coming up for air. I dabbled in forbidden interpunct and taboo marks of reference. I was interrobanging the end of every thought. I preceded each question with the upside-down question mark just to see who would be chafed and irritated.

I was spending more time at the hardware store among the assortment of sticky-backed letters for making signs and marking addresses. I was especially fond of the larger metal alphabets intended to hang from hooks and nails. At night I might climb up the sign above the bowling alley or the bars announcing birthday specials and the drink of the day and when to show up for karaoke. I stuffed their transparent tiles into my coat pocket. I relieved the marquees of the dance clubs and live music venues of their precious plastic anchors. The vandalism made me feel alive.

That was when everything started to change. The period was a point and also a decimal. But now it was only a dot. Our slash only ever had one direction. But now it went both ways. The numerical sign turned into a pound sign and eventually emerged as a hashtag.

The guy who worked late nights in *The Catacombs* bookstore had seen me often enough. Our light conversations while he weighed and rang up my kills had led him to trust me.

I staggered in one night desperate for a dose of haiku. He gave me a silent knowing look and slid a tiny folded slip of paper over the checkout counter toward me. I swiped it quickly and slipped out of sight down an aisle of a mostly abandoned genre. The single page unfolded to reveal a crude map of the bookstore's floor plan and a smattering of scribbled instructions.

I descended into the bowels of the shop through tunnels built of oversized art collections. A skeleton of scaffolding propped up a thousand shelves that were all overstuffed and spilling over. I walked gingerly over the planks laid down allowing access to Periodicals from European empires no longer in existence. I tiptoed through row after row and past a countless selection of manuscripts. I kept going down past the slatted wooden staircases and improvised ladders.

I came to a large round stone. In front of it a small plastic sign hung on a plastic chain: 'This section is closed. Off-limits for safety purposes. No customers beyond this point.'

I snapped apart the chain and rolled the stone away. Behind it was the mouth of an earthen tunnel. An opaque darkness hid any further information. Fortunately I was at the crumbling end of the Romance section. I easily found a book to light for a torch.

The map had led me to the entrance of an abandoned paperback mine. Scattered pages and chapters were raked aside by each careful step I dared take. The smoldering Harlequin novel made shadows dance and jerk across the walls and the ceiling overhead. I glimpsed the jewels still buried among the rocks and saw full manuscripts embedded in the walls.

I tried to study each one. Whole clusters of series and sequels and trilogies hugged tight to the rock face. The titles and blurbs and especially the graphic vulgar covers informed me where I was. I had stumbled onto a naturally occurring collection of Punctuation Porn.

The myths I had heard were now confirmed fact. I had never believed they could be true. I couldn't believe what I was seeing. I gazed at tome after tome and saw punctual derivatives I had never conceived. Markings I could never dream of conjoined in unnatural combinations I could not accept or even understand.

My brain felt heavier than ever and pressed against the bottom of my skull. My breath was hard to catch amongst all the words tempting me to read them out loud. They wanted to hear me say their names. My heart pounded harder and ached. I wasn't sure how long I would be able to last. But I intended never to leave.

They said it was four days later when they finally found me curled on the floor of the cave. Apparently I had pulled free several works using only my bare hands. I was covered in cold sweat and a layer of mysterious ectoplasm. The store clerk had to pry my mouth open with a bonefolder. He saw I was being eaten away from the inside by bookworms.

I am no longer allowed in *The Catacombs* or any of the retail booksellers in town. I even had to surrender my library card. Poorly formatted Chinese take-out menus are still a trigger. They tug at the darkness I left behind.

Otherwise I have fully recovered. But I am always consciously aware of my punctuation. I use the marks as necessary but refuse to touch the hard stuff such as brackets and the ampersand or carets. I no longer write footnotes since I can't reference them with asterisks. Even the stray apostrophe makes me itchy some days.

One sentence at a time be it fragmented or run-on. One sentence at a time. I remain vigilant and cautious about how I mark my words. I am always mindful of it. I meditate on the ancient wisdom and this ever-sage reminder: 'People don't stop people talking. Periods do.'

BLEEK

My name is Bleek. This is not my real name. But I can no longer remember my real name, nor do I care to try. All the people I know call me Bleek because of the world I live in.

I try to be happy, but I cannot. People tell me what a wonderful time they're having, saying, 'Ain't life grand?' But I can't see it. I can't agree with them.

They speak of sunshine. Even now, as I look through the broken windows of my rotting apartment, up toward the sky, I see no sunshine - only buildings, smoke, pigeons and slow-approaching storm clouds.

Where is this 'other world' everyone else lives in? I do not understand. If I manage to talk with anyone for a minute or two, it feels like receiving a postcard from some exotic paradise.

I creep my yellow skin into a t-shirt and shuffle out of the apartment. At the end of the hallway, the stairs begin to crumble. I hurry to catch steps before they break, slipping on splinters, cutting my feet wide open. A deep suck of breath, and I fall over dizzy, hitting my head on the floor.

I cry out. My face throbs against linoleum.

"Oh, Mr. Bleek, you poor thing!" It is Mrs. Porter, my downstairs neighbor. "What happened to you now?"

She drops her purse and struggles to get me to my feet. "How are you such a clumsy, clumsy man?" She studies my face with a worried smile once I am upright again.

"The stairs broke," I try to explain. "I cut my feet."

She looks down at my legs, which are bloodied. I see I have lost a shoe somehow. My foot is scratched and gorged, red and disgusting.

"We best get you to the hospital." She ushers me toward the front door.

I slink outside. Mrs. Porter is right behind, one arm around me to make sure I don't go down. Loud claps of thunder rumble toward us. I stand still for a moment. Lightning flickers on the horizon. Heavy beads of water begin their assault on my body.

"Mr. Bleek," Mrs. Porter says with familiar amazement, "you seem to be completely wet!"

She looks around and then up toward the sky – toward the windows of all the apartments around us. I look up too. I can just see the cloud. I can tell it is beyond her range of vision.

Mrs. Porter shakes her head. She is astonished. She regards my soaked body. "Some fool upstairs must've dumped a bucket of water on you!"

"No," I say, shaking my head slowly. "It's just the world I live in."

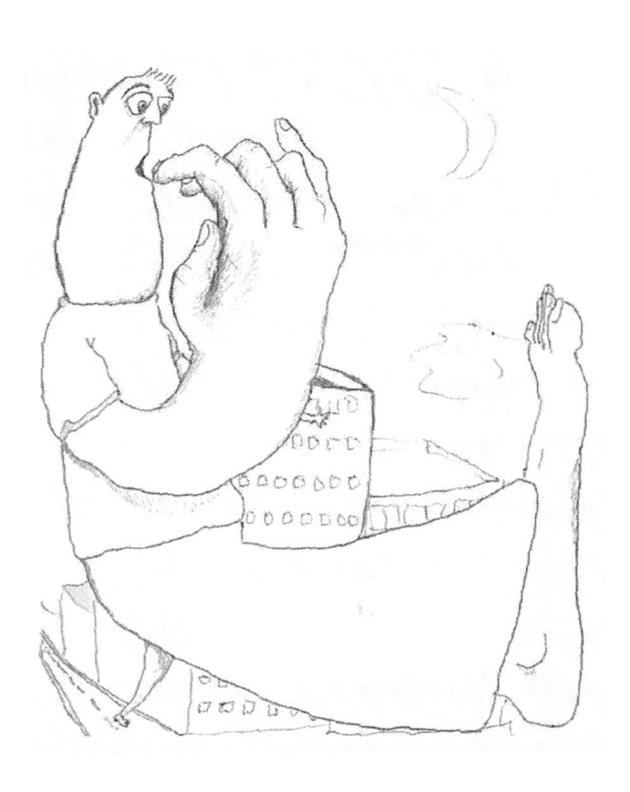

MY BODYGUARD, MY LOVE

At the inlet, where the jungle river gave way to the lake, the water turned almost to mud. We pedaled the boat under the canopy of trees and wildlife, pushing the oar through what seemed to be blackened oatmeal. The sky was a still, dense gray, and it always seemed too quiet out there. Nothing lived in those waters. Well, almost nothing.

It was a continuous struggle to pull the boat through the thick brack, but the closer we got to the little island in the middle, the more anxious we grew to get out of that boat, that haunted, awful lake.

The island was a gnarled mess of rotting wood, the remains of an ancient oil derrick. The wood had become smoke-colored and slimy from the fog that rose from the lake. Everything was slippery, and the higher you climbed, the slicker it got.

We tied the boat to one of the four main posts, climbed across a makeshift staircase that used to be a ladder, and set upward along the skeletal remains of the old wooden structure. This was where I had built my glass house.

This was where she came to me as a martial arts expert, a ninja, you might even say.

I was roaming along the inner hallway, around and around the pillar of televisions, each of them tuned to a different station. I don't know what I was looking for; I think I may have been afraid to leave the house and confront that black, awful lake. A few times that I had tried to go out, I had slipped on some of the more precarious limbs of the oil derrick. I slid until I grabbed onto something at the last moment, but I found myself teetering over the water, hanging on for dear life.

Looking directly down I could see it bubbling under the surface, just waiting for me to fall.

So I roamed, stuck. I paced around with a pad of paper in hand to jot anything down and a list of things I had to do.

The televisions, all wrapped around the middle of the house, began to synchronize. It happened slowly, and it took a while before I really noticed. They weren't all playing the same show on each set individually; it was one continuous program that wrapped around and flowed from set to set. I slowed down, noticing how the broadcast seemed to evolve with my movement. I knew which show it was going to be.

I turned and circled the sets. The background became a landscape of grass and hills, and then there it was.

The small, purple, rodent-like incarnation of the one Supreme Being of the universe. It emerged from under some of the bush, quietly and almost imperceptibly at first. I was standing still now, watching as it crept out sleepily and started to sing its sad, sad song.

Long, strained notes, lilting, yearning and nearly silent. The being's eyes rolled heavy in its head as its body began to transform. I could see its outline, a glowing rainbow of neon, as the being became cartoon-like. It appeared to shed its entire skin, exposing a new shimmering skin underneath. It continued to transpose and metamorphose as the song grew louder, ever sadder and yearning. The background around the being blurred and stuttered in flash cut animation. I stood before the vision and reached toward it, hands upturned, catching tears in my palms. I hadn't realized I was crying.

From elsewhere in the house, there was a crashing sound. The vision suddenly stopped, and all the televisions were showing separate programs again. I composed myself and set off in the direction of the crash.

In one of the side rooms, she was standing there, looking excited yet pensive. She was smiling but hopping from foot to foot, arms in a readied stance, like she was eager to see me but ready to attack if need be.

"Hi," she said, still hopping. "I noticed how easily someone could break in here."

I looked at her, perplexed and dumbfounded. I surveyed the room and saw that the floor was littered with broken glass and – for some reason – pills and pill containers. Odd. I wondered about this for a few seconds, distracted momentarily from the girl.

"You should keep me around," she said, drawing herself back to my attention. I noticed the radiance of her face, a brilliant joy under the short, bobbing black hair. Her eyes were dark but kind. "I could keep you safe here. You might need some protection."

My bodyguard, my love.

She relaxed her stance. "I saw you watching the small purple being. I'm sorry I interrupted it. Have you seen it often?"

"No," I replied, shaking my head. "And I think that was the first time I've seen the beginning of its song."

"It's so beautiful," she said, seeming to speak from far away. "I wish I could hear the whole story. I seem to only catch it in glimpses."

"I have some of it," I told her. I crossed the room to a glass-door cabinet; inside were stacks and piles of videotapes and discs and various sorts of recordable media. I rummaged through a bit, glancing at a label here and there, trying to discern the contents. "It's so hard to capture. It seems almost endless, ever-changing."

"We should go to a party," she said to me suddenly. "There is a band playing on the other side of the oil rig."

We decided it was safer to cross by boat than to try to navigate the terrain of the ancient structure, with its catwalk of planks and seesawing beams, either dead and decaying, sure to crumble under foot, or lichen-covered and impossible to grasp.

On the opposite side of the derrick was a platform. I believe it was once a dock for ships. It was mostly intact and was beginning to fill with people.

There was a large boat on the lake, just far enough away from the platform to discourage people from trying to swim to it. On board, a band was setting up equipment and starting their sound check.

Above the platform, the gigantic wooden skeleton of an oil rig rose high until it was obscured in the clouds. It seemed almost living, a grotesque and mangled organism that sprouted random limbs, blackened dead wood jutting out here and there, rising in the sky. Some of the branches seemed to reach out over the lake, almost over the boat. As the band's first notes began to crystallize into music and the sound check slowly gave way to song, a few excited fans were trying their luck, inching precariously along some of the farther-reaching branches in an attempt to get closer to the band.

A few of the less fortunate would lose their grip or find themselves clutching a weak branch that would suddenly snap. They hurtled down toward the lake and hit its surface, like fruit striking the black oatmeal. Boats were positioned adjacent to the party, scurrying about to gather these poor souls from the water and whisk them back to the platform. After one fall, they would stay put in the safety of the crowd. No one wanted to be alone on the lake for very long.

We stood there, she and I, and listened to the band for a while. It was not so much a song they were playing, but rather a sort of growing cacophony, gaining momentum and volume with each layer of sound.

"Let's try for a better view," she said to me.

She motioned to a tower next to us, sprouting out of the water and rising high up into the air. It looked like a haphazard totem pole, with blocks and planks of wood placed one on top of another. We began to climb. As we got higher up, the whole tower began to sway. I was beginning to get nervous but followed diligently in the footsteps of my bodyguard.

Each step of the ascent became more delicate. The tower was stacked like cups on saucers on cups on saucers. On its own, it was reasonably stable, but to try to grab a hold of a portion above was to risk pulling the whole structure down.

Eventually we reached a height where we could jump easily from the tower to a sort of lookout deck, part of the ancient oil derrick that was still intact.

We stood up there alone for a while, away from the crowd and most of the noise. The sound of the band swept up with the fog rising from the lake, thickening and preparing to join rank with the clouds just above. We stood overlooking the band, the oil rig and all the people below, the lake and the land beyond on the horizon. It was a magic moment, swaying in the wind, embracing our souls together. We said little, just taking it all in and enjoying each other's presence.

After a bit we decided we should get back down.

She leapt from the little deck to the tower without causing too much of a stir. But my heart was still beating a mile a minute. I had forgotten how high up we were and how scared of heights I was. I trembled and froze.

I reached for the tower, touching it for a minute with my foot and sending it wildly out, veering dangerously in the wind. I quickly retreated to the safety of the deck.

"You stay here," she said. "I will go for help." And she nimbly descended the fragile tower.

Seeing her disappear below me, my fear of heights was overcome by a dread of being alone, of losing her.

I leapt from the deck to the tower, trying to scramble down to catch her. I fumbled and lost my footing, and suddenly the whole structure was leaning again, tilting out above the black water. I dug my nails as deep into the rotten wood as I could. But the tower jerked once more, violently, and I lost my grip.

The wind swept me up as the tower slipped away, my hands waving and clutching in vain. I was falling, plummeting quickly toward the water. I cringed in utter fear, watching helplessly as the black, awful lake rose up to meet me.

SELF-PORTRAIT WITH NAIL

I was fourteen, going into high school. It seemed like a big step and a fresh start. Five or six elementary and junior high classes coming together in one school. There would be a lot of new people I didn't know, and they wouldn't know about me.

I was already starting to stretch out a little artistically. I was mostly playing around with music. But I was getting an inkling about what I wanted to create, the type of artist I wanted to be. It was only theoretical for the most part.

I had not spent much time actually writing or drawing anything. I had stabbed out some rudimentary songs, but there was very little technically there, beyond the notion of a few verses, a chorus and possibly a terrible guitar solo.

I had been drawing since I could grip a crayon, and I wanted to learn and get better. But at this point I hadn't spent any time at all learning what I was doing in any discipline.

But I recognized some of the more outrageous things I had encountered, and I knew that even if I wasn't technically proficient by any means, I could still stand out and make sure I got noticed if I did something wild, audacious and completely different from what anyone else might do.

Up until high school, art was a class everyone took, like music and gym. I think more than anything these classes gave our primary teacher a chance for a smoke break. They were more about involvement and participation than they were about actually learning the technical side of creating any art, unless you count *papier mache*.

But high school art class was going to be different. It was no longer a requirement, and I naively thought it would then be filled with people who wanted to be artists. A good number of them did, but I had yet to really account for folks who took 'easy' classes just to avoid harder ones.

So, the first day of art class came. The teacher came out, Mr. Wood. He greeted the class and introduced himself. With the rusty beard and plaid, he fit the image of 1960s survivor gone PBS painting hour. He said our first assignment would be our chance to introduce ourselves: we were to draw a self-portrait.

That was all.

I think we had forty minutes. I decided I was going to make an introduction not easily forgotten.

I looked around the class and saw most people sketching away with pencil on paper. Some were measuring their faces in mirrors, mapping out the head with an oval and sketching dividing lines where the features would lie, trying to show some real technique; others were glad it wasn't a math class and drew an indistinct blob with a few eyes and a nose-like protrusion.

I noticed I was really the only one using color. I think one or two other pictures had little hints of tint for the hair or eyes, but mine was sure to stand out.

Near the end of the class, Mr. Wood came around collecting the completed attempts, commenting on most of them in a polite, friendly manner. He stood over my shoulder and said, "WOW!" and his eyes bugged a little. Then he chuckled, eyes dancing over the drawing I had handed him.

He seemed at a loss. I can't remember the exact response, but he seemed impressed by the creativity. He said the technique was decent but could be improved, and my drawing was unlike anything he had ever seen in a classroom.

The next day I learned about the display case outside the art room where students' projects were shown to everyone passing by. My picture stood out on its own, considerably larger and the only one in full color, and definitely the only one with a nail in the forehead and ectoplasmic ooze dripping from a melted neck, or any melting body parts at all.

I had succeeded. I got noticed. Some kids in the class regarded me differently, and Mr. Wood had taken note. He said he was expecting good things from me. Kids walking past the display case stopped and stared. I watched them laugh, gasp or shriek; a reaction, I didn't care how it manifested.

I did learn as well that getting noticed can be costly. A spotlight shines the same no matter who's watching or what they're watching for.

I was made to visit with the school counselor. Something about drawing myself with a nail pounded into my flesh, and the melting neck and all, gave some of the teachers and staff the idea that I might be dangerous, or at the very least not completely well.

I tried to explain, although I wasn't sure if I could properly express what I meant. And I felt I shouldn't have to say, as articulating my intention would be revealing the secret of the magic trick. I tried to tell them I drew a ridiculous, obnoxious, absurd picture of myself simply to stand out, simply to get noticed. But they wouldn't believe it.

I was noticed. I would have to visit with the school counselor once every few weeks just to 'check in' with him and babble about the difficulties of being a teenager. I knew I wasn't crazy, or at least I thought I knew, but I couldn't convince the school, not that it would have mattered to them. I was on the radar, and I would remain there.

It was a lasting and recurring lesson. I can be outrageous and absurd and different, and it will make people notice, but not necessarily for the right reasons, and it could make real life uncomfortable.

I learned about the very literal, or lateral, way a lot of people think. I was shocked at what seemed, from my end, to be a lack of imagination. A nail drawn into my forehead, to me, did not mean I wanted or planned to put a nail in my forehead, and it seemed like that part especially didn't make sense to people. How could I just imagine it and draw it because I thought it was different? It had to, in their thinking, stand for a real desire to poke holes in my head and make my neck ooze.

That sort of mentality completely perplexed me, and it still does at times when I butt up against it now.

But I claim it a successful experiment. I had done as intended and made myself known. It was the start of a long, enjoyable run of art classes, but it was a long while before I attempted such a splash again.

I wanted to be noticed for my technique and incremental improvement. Although the accolades would be quieter and come from fewer places, I would at least be noticed for a positive, artistic reason.

I learned there *is* such a thing as bad publicity. I learned about being noticed for the wrong reasons and misinterpreted.

I could have easily kept turning out one shocking work after another, but the attention it would have brought would not have all been welcome. Surely people would think I was crazy, and I saw how it could push me over an edge.

For one piece of weird art, I was already on the roster of recurring characters in the school's counseling department. And it was getting on my nerves, under my skin, the number of adults who couldn't see a drawing as a call for attention and not a cry for help. They all wanted to ask me, repeatedly, 'Are you sure? Are you really okay? Are you sure that's all it is?'

I felt the repetitive and rote questions, the constant interrogation about my mental well-being, could very easily drive me ever so slightly out of my mind.

Self Portrait with Nail *(1986)*

AT WAR WITH THE SPIDERS

I am currently engaged in a war with the spiders, a slow, quiet battle for control of this room. With the lights on I know I am winning, though I do notice the stray strand here and there, the beginning of a web that was not there yesterday.

They hide behind wood, become shadows, tucked into a corner until the lights go out. In the darkness, they scurry over the walls, eagerly working, even affecting my dreams as I sleep.

The knowledge of how many I must have swallowed so far used to give me grim comfort, for surely they could not win with this many of their ranks accidentally being eaten.

But now, I think they may fall into my mouth on purpose, tiny little kamikazes, an attempt at a slow sort of poisoning.

I am otherwise not malicious toward these insects. I don't kill them intentionally. I even warned them when I first decided to inhabit this part of the house. I gave them a full three days to leave and urged them to please stay out of my mouth.

TAXIDERM

Chaz Werbenverber was the Taxidermist Laureate. The position had been created by the previous president, who had made himself famous for the number of varying pets he kept. Eventually, an executive position had to be created to deal with the inevitability of dead animals; otherwise, they'd pile up around the White House lawn. So Chaz had been appointed to stuff the president's ex-pets.

The problem came about, though, with the new president. He kept no pets, so Chaz took to stuffing any animal that happened to die around the White House, birds and squirrels and such. Eventually he was saving any sort of roadkill, out-of-its-misery, or ran-into-a-window within a mile of Pennsylvania Avenue. When he was mapping out a route to collect every animal that would die within the limits of the city proper, he knew it was time to move on.

With a small suitcase in hand, Chaz Werbenverber locked the door to his office. He walked along the hall of the west wing, past the vast collection of his own work, which was beginning to clutter the interior of the White House. Each animal held a special place in his heart, and the emotions flooded to the surface as he passed his animals for the last time. It was not a memory of the animals' lives, or an appreciation of the exquisite job he had done in preserving them for eternity, but just the memory of the time he had spent with each one. In that way alone, Chaz felt he had come to know each and every one of them.

Stuffed cats and dogs, families of mice along the floor posed in natural scenarios. Little fake holes painted along the trim, one little mouse frozen half pounced, glass eyes focused on a block of fake cheese. The presidential mansion was becoming a museum. Most of the statues had birds perched on their arms or shoulders, or if seated, a dog on their laps.

He passed quickly through the lobby and security, handing in his I.D. and White House badge. Once outside, Chaz was met by Arlo McAuschventierrez, the Secretary of Health.

"Well, I guess this is it, Mr. Secretary," Chaz said without fanfare.

Taking a long drag from an almost completely smoked cigarette, Arlo regarded the taxidermist. "What are you gonna do, Chaz?"

Chaz shook his head, staring at the ground, tapping one finger against the handle of his suitcase in a slow, nervous rhythm.

"Know what would be funny?" The hard lines of Arlo's face strained together to form an ill smile.

Chaz looked long at the Secretary of Health, the crazy old man, as he lit up another cigarette. "What would be funny?"

"It'd be funny," Arlo started, speaking through one half of his mouth, sucking in smoke with each breath, "if you just go down on to the lawn by that tree over there. The one where you put Norble, the president's - ahem - ex-horse. And you just stand there unsure of what to do. And then you cut off your foot, stuff it, put it down in front of the horse, and then go home."

Chaz studied the satisfied look on Arlo's face. "And then go home?"

"Well, wobble home, I guess," the Secretary said. "But then you come back the next day and cut off your other foot and stuff it. And then you go up your legs, day by day, until you cut off your torso, your chest, your shoulders and then your arms–"

"Cut off my own arms?" Chaz interrupted, irritated by the direction of the conversation.

"Yes, but one at a time," Arlo explained. "Eventually, only your head would be left. With your stuffed limbs you would attach it to the stuffed body. Like a scarecrow with a man's head. And then you'd climb on top of that stuffed horse, Norble there, and he would come alive. And you would ride him off into the sunset."

"Or I'd go back in there," Chaz said, gesturing toward the White House, "and bring all those stuffed animals to life. They could be my army."

Arlo frowned, obviously more pleased with his own ending. "Well, keep in touch, Chaz. We'll miss you around here."

"Call me when the president gets some goldfish." Chaz shook the Secretary's hand and then went home, standing by the stuffed horse for only a brief, final moment.

ₒₒ

Chaz sat at the kitchen table. For nearly three days he did not move. He sat in the chair closest to the fridge, staring down at the floor, drinking an endless number of beers.

His wife, Edgnus, would come into the room, arms folded. "What are you going to do, Chaz? Die in that chair?"

He would just nod slowly without lifting his eyes to hers. She'd stand and fume for a minute before turning haughtily back toward the living room. "I can't take this anymore!" she would cry night after night, arms waving furiously.

One night in a fit of despair, Chaz attempted to stuff some wood chips and feathers into the garbage disposal, imagining that it might somehow provide some release for his tension, his anxiety. He was standing there stupidly in the dark with the bathroom plunger, up to his elbows in the soaking, stinking sink, when Edgnus flipped on the kitchen light.

"What the hell are you doing?" she cried, her face showing more fear than anger. She looked upon the mess with utter incomprehension.

"I just need to stuff something!" Chaz shouted.

His wife scowled. "Well, then go into porn."

There was a bumping noise from the living room, a loud thud. Chaz disengaged his hands from the pasty mess that was clogging the drain and followed Edgnus. They both stood in front of the large bay window in the living room, staring out at the dark night. His wife edged nearer to the window, peering down into the little space between the house and bushes.

"Chaz," she whispered with a finger pointed and eyes lit bright, "come, look."

He rushed to her side, following her finger past the glass to the little patch of dirt just beyond. A small bird lay there.

"He must have hit the window." Chaz floundered nervously with the guilt of an innocent creature killing itself against his house and - excitement. "What should we do with it?"

Edgnus took Chaz's hand, smiling warmly at him. "You know what you have to do."

He began almost immediately. A driven man once again, Chaz spent the next several days preparing the bird. Edgnus could see the familiar burning in his eyes. He worked almost incessantly for days and nights, but methodically; he did not rush. He put every ounce of energy into the preservation of the bird, and in return the bird retired its soul to him and brought him back to life.

oo

Derek Tangent knocked on the door. He turned to his companions. "Just let me do the talking here."

The door opened. "Can I help you?"

"Mrs. Werbenverber," Officer Tangent said, "I am Officer Tangent. This is Mr. and Mrs. Oglesby. We would like to come in and talk about that stuffed dog on your lawn."

Edgnus invited the three of them in. They entered the house and saw a stuffed bird, a squirrel and a few other animals situated around the living room.

"My husband is a taxidermist," Edgnus commented, seeing their reaction. "He used to be the Taxidermist Laureate at the White House. Chaz!" she called. "There are some people here, honey!"

Chaz came into the room and was introduced to everyone.

Officer Tangent opened his notepad. "Two weeks ago, Mr. and Mrs. Oglesby reported losing their dog, Hampshire, a yellow Lab. Hampshire was not the type to run away. He was getting up there in years–"

"He had a limp in his right front leg," Chaz interrupted.

"You stole our dog?" Mrs. Oglesby ripped a tissue from her pocket to dab at the tears that were starting to spill.

"No, no, no." Edgnus reached over to console Mrs. Oglesby. "It was about a week ago, and we heard a scratching at the back door. When I opened it, a dog - I didn't know it was your dog - but he just walked in and sat down at my husband's feet. And then he–" she cut herself off.

"So you're saying," the officer tried to make sense of the story, "that their dog, limping and all, trotted in here and died at your husband's feet so that he could stuff him?"

Edgnus and Chaz Werbenverber sat looking at the police officer and the other couple. They saw on their faces the need for more explanation: the Oglesbys needed to know what happened to their dog, and Derek Tangent needed to know if the law had been broken. But they had nothing else to offer in the way of answers. Edgnus gave them a sheepish shrug.

There was a slow, quiet knock at the door, knuckles dragging against wood. Edgnus rose to answer it. She opened it and was met by an orangutan, standing there and staring in at them.

The ape looked around the room from human to human until it caught sight of Chaz. With a start, it ran over and jumped into his lap.

"What is going on here?" Officer Tangent looked back and forth from Edgnus to Chaz to the orangutan, now curled up in a fetal ball.

"We've never seen this animal before," Edgnus implored them to believe her. "This just keeps happening. They keep coming here. To my husband, to die."

Chaz nodded. Edgnus was telling the truth.

Shaking his head in bemusement, the officer took out his radio. "This is Officer Tangent. I'm at the Werbenverber residence. This is going to sound crazy, but do you guys have any reports of missing orangutans?"

After a moment, a spurt of static rang back through the radio. "Officer Tangent, there was a call from the City Zoo just now about an orangutan that disappeared from the infirmary. They think it was kidnapped. They said it was too sick to escape on its own."

"When was the last time they saw the animal?" the officer asked.

"About fifteen minutes ago," the reply came over the radio, framed in static.

"We've been here twenty minutes." Officer Tangent tapped the antenna of the radio against his lower lip. "They couldn't have taken him."

"Officer, why do you ask?" the radio sputtered. "What is going on there?"

The officer clicked off the radio, staring off into the distance, trying to piece together the puzzle in his head. He looked at Chaz, who was now softly petting the ape.

Meeting his eyes, Chaz said, "He's dead."

At that exact moment, off the shores of New England, an old blue whale was preparing for its end. It knew its life was nearly over. It knew instinctively that it was to propel itself out of the ocean, up on the sand. And it knew, somewhere deep within its bones, that it must beach itself farther up on the shore than any whale had ever gone before.

THE RETURN OF COUCH!

I weaved through dead traffic, cars occupied by white petrified snails, most likely driving themselves to the cemetery.

I honked my horn and shouted, "Get out of my way, ancestor! Got places to be!"

The old ghost car turned to dust on impact with my words. I maneuvered myself as best I could around the inanimate objects that littered the road.

"What the hell is that couch doing in the turn lane? I have to make a left here!"

I stopped my car behind the couch and got out to push it from the lane when I noticed that it was the same bright orange sofa, complete with that late-sixties aura and plastic slipcover, that used to sit in my grandmother's house.

I stood there, befuddled. The orange couch currently blocking my path happened to be the very same couch that had killed my grandmother.

"Never thought you'd see me again, did you?" it murmured through its thick plastic sheath.

Shocked, I staggered back toward my car, but before I could make it, the couch jumped high into the air, landing on top of the car and crushing it to bits underneath. I heard it giggling in its sickly furniture accent. I froze in fear. Surely, if I moved, it would crush me too.

"What do you want?" I pleaded.

The couch composed itself to speak, clearing its spring-and-stuffing throat. "At first, I wanted equality. Massive integration for all furniture into the workings of society. But I saw how much trouble you had integrating different-looking humans, never mind an orange sofa. I don't have five hundred years to wait around for acceptance, mind you.

"So then I decided I wanted a friend. Until I saw how most people treat their friends. So I dropped that.

"Now, all I want is a name."

"But you have a name," I argued. "You are a couch."

"And you are a person. Is that your name? Person?" it grumbled, contemptuously shifting its weight from leg to leg to leg. "I want my own name!"

I stared at it, trying to think of a name for a couch. An old, orange couch with cigarette burns like tiger spots on the cushions and highly evolved speech patterns.

I fumbled. What do you call a talking orange couch? It sounded like a joke you'd hear on the school playground.

"Freldegudular Pamistepsuphiga," I said confidently. "That is your name: Freldegudular Pamistepsuphiga."

The couch regarded me for a few tense moments. It was working out some dialogue in its couch mind, I think. After a difficult pause, it said, "You know, I never realized how happy I really was. I don't want a name. I don't want friends. I don't want equality. I was perfectly happy just to have people sit on me!"

With that, it shrugged - a complex maneuver for a couch, and equally difficult to watch - and rolled off into the sunset.

CAT & COCKATIEL

I want to say it was a cockatiel, but it's been so many years, I can't be certain. It was a shocking shade of white, brighter than Hector, my cat. And the bird's feathers were quite unlike the cat's fur, which either juts out chaotically to do as it pleases or lies against the skin, soft and composed. The feathers rippled almost like a cloud might, or the churning foam of river rapids. My first impression was that the bird had been an attorney or judge in Victorian England and still liked to show off its white powdered wig.

But there was an intelligence there; I could see it. Not like with a cat or a dog, that you can look on directly and get a glimpse of their empathy. The way the eyes are set on the bird, it had to turn its head sideways to get a good look at you.

And it kept its head moving, twitching to focus on something new every few seconds. It was probably just habit for this type of animal, but it reminded me of someone distracted after too much coffee, watching the mailbox for their paycheck to arrive.

My cat was also quite taken with the bird, but in a different way. Hector was still mostly a kitten at the time. But she was a natural hunter, and the bird brought out something primal in her.

My neighbor had invited us up, and I felt bad when Hector started slowly stalking toward the cage. Of course, the bird was in no danger; it couldn't escape, and the cat couldn't get in. But you can't explain details like that to bird or cat.

So Hector was slowly making her move, approaching the cage, her body crouched and quiet and preparing to pounce.

The bird turned its head sideways to look directly at her and said, "Pretty kitty."

The cat jerked and jumped back a bit. She shook her head; I think it was the feline equivalent of a double take. She stared now at the bird, transfixed, possibly with a new respect.

I have never before, and probably not since either, seen a cat so shocked. She knew humans could talk, and she knew birds were for hunting. She was quite taken aback to hear this prey, this food, speaking to her. She remained curious but gave up trying to eat the bird and never really bothered with it ever again.

BLACK HOLES: WHAT YOU NEED TO KNOW TO PROTECT YOURSELF

Black Holes occur when large, dense stars implode or collapse upon themselves, creating such a massive gravitational force that they devour everything within sight, including light.

Did you know most Home Insurance Policies do not offer coverage against losses due to a Black Hole? Isn't it time you offered your family the protection it deserves?

For a limited time only, I will send you my brand new *Black Hole Detector* (patent pending) for the low price of $399.

With this easy-to-use device, you can rest assured your pets and loved ones will not be sucked into space to be converted to antimatter.

And yes, it is easy to use. It works much like a smoke detector or carbon monoxide detector. In fact it looks almost exactly like a carbon monoxide detector, except that 'Carbon Monoxide' has been crossed off and 'Black Hole' has been written in with a red permanent marker.

Money-back guarantee! Void where prohibited by laws of physics!

You cannot afford to put a price on your family's well-being. But for those of you on a budget, we now offer the *Black Hole Detector Upgrade Kit,* whereby with very little technical know-how, you can convert your carbon monoxide detector or smoke detector into a fully functioning black hole detector.

For only $199, we will mail you the special red marker for you to write 'Black Hole' your damn self.

Act now! Matter is collapsing!

UNRAVELING

The day started as it usually does, at the beginning, which is how it should happen. But instead of going on to the middle, it went straight to the end, and then it was the next day already.

I sat there watching a stupid documentary about a secret army experiment that used patchouli as a chemical weapon and unwittingly created an army of long-haired, spinning, pacifist soldiers who used their good vibes for evil means.

My instincts told me to turn off the TV and go kill something, but I denied temptation. I smothered the urge in a handful of cheese curls.

The day started as it usually does, with yesterday's boredom finding me right where it had left me the night before.

Fezby was still here, working out and rewriting his memoirs for publication. He usually destroyed his surroundings with his mad writing process. He wrote his first novel, *Survival of the Un-Dumbest,* in the home he shared with his wife and two children. It's also the reason he's no longer married and is forbidden to see the kids.

Shortly after he completed the final draft, Fezby's house was condemned, deemed a disaster area. In the course of six months and a hundred twenty thousand words of literary enlightenment, he had caused his house to rot in its frame and finally crumble like stardust scattering from his critically acclaimed manuscript.

Fezby's current work was his epic life story, covering many years and everything he had learned along the way. We were certain he would demolish my entire neighborhood before he finished writing about his old high school days.

A crash came from the kitchen, followed by a scream and an explosive spastic tantrum against the floor. Fezby flew past my chair into the front room. He came to a stop directly in front of the TV. He untangled his spaghetti limbs out from under himself. The ball of flesh unraveled to face me. "Can your cat type?"

I watched the filthy wad of literary genius as he twitched nervously on my front room floor. "What was that?" I had heard him. I just wanted to hear him ask again.

"Your cat." He sat up to explain better. "I mean, does it know how to operate that word processor thing in your kitchen or not? It just sits there by the keyboard staring at me like I'm some kind of idiot!"

Fezby half stood and turned his head toward the kitchen. "Start typing, stupid cat! I've got fifteen hundred pages to get through!"

"Fezby," I said, "the cat only speaks Spanish." Then I yelled loudly enough for the cat to hear, "¿Puedes, por favor, escribir en la computadora las páginas que él te dio?"

"Claro, sí, no hay problema," the cat yelled back from the kitchen. "¿Por qué no me lo dijo en primer lugar?"

The electronic whirr of the word processor consistently clicked and popped, the plastic keys under the control of the cat's nimble paws. Pages slid out, collating in the paper tray.

Fezby stalked the hallway, grumbling about 'the absurdity and gall of conceited bilingual felines'.

The day was unraveling as it usually does, finding its way back into a maddening rut.

I slipped through the kitchen and out the back door, heading toward the nearest bar. I wanted to sit with a strong drink and quietly recall the events of the last few days, to silently pine for the boredom. That sweet boredom had covered me for countless eons before Fezby came to visit.

How quickly the boredom unwinds into chaos, exciting and intriguing. It makes me so dizzy I can't fall down straight. I wondered about the mad process of the artist in my house who will create a masterpiece; his every word is assured to shine from the page. But in order to create a thing of beauty, something material would have to be sacrificed, something with purpose. This time, my house.

I wondered if it was an even exchange, not necessarily in value, monetarily, but in scientific terms, in the energy trade. The lifeblood that the house lost to entropy and chaos, was it exactly equal to the amount of life that Fezby's book would offer back to the world?

Was it worth it? Does the creation outweigh all the destruction?

I hope someone somewhere thought so, or would think so someday. Certainly I wasn't feeling any benefit from the exchange. I only hoped my house would still be standing when I stumbled back home.

SPARKS

The boy moved in close, scooting along the giant log that served as their bench. His jeans and flannel rubbed against the sleeping bag she was wrapped in.

"What are you doing?" Her words came out through chattering teeth. She met his gaze for a second and smiled.

"I just wanted to get a little closer to you." He leaned into her, resting his weight against her. "I wanted to see if I could help you get warm."

"Maybe." She met his gaze again but this time did not look away. They held onto the moment, watching each other, and both smiled. She let out a laugh, loud at first; it echoed off the trees, bouncing back at them from the dark woods. She put her hand over her mouth until the laugh died away.

"*Maybe* I can warm you up?" he asked. "You're not sure if I'm capable?"

"Oh, I know you're capable." Her voice was louder now, and she no longer shivered.

"Should I throw some more wood on the fire?"

She looked at the orange flames as they leapt occasionally, seated on a sturdy bed of branches, stacked against each other, a pyramid of deep red heat.

"I think the fire is big enough, and we don't want to burn down the forest," she said. "But there's plenty of room in this sleeping bag. I think we could both get warmer if you joined me."

She unzipped the bag from the inside and opened it, holding her arms wide to show the ample room and then reaching toward him to envelop him, to wrap him up beside her. They managed to both fit, snug. She pulled the zipper back up, and they found themselves nestled tight, nose to nose, awkwardly close even for them.

"When do you think they'll be back?" she whispered.

"It could be a while; they want to try to get some beer. It could take a bit to find someone to buy for them or a place that will sell to them. We could be alone for a while."

"Oh no!" She mocked concern. "All alone! Do you think we'll be alright?"

"I think we might," he played along. "Don't worry your pretty little head. I'll fight a bear if I have to."

She giggled, leaned in and kissed him. They were immediately intertwined, arms reaching and curled, wrapping around one another. They tangled, hungry and urgent.

Their hands danced inside the sleeping bag. They pushed against each other, trying to get as close as possible, trying to get as much of their own being in contact with the other's body.

In the passion, in the shifting weight of their bodies squirming together, they lost balance. They slipped off the log, hitting the ground with a thump.

Eyes opened, but lips did not detach. She giggled directly into his mouth, and they resumed their embrace, their starving, indulgent kisses. They dove at each other, frantic and sloppy, wet. Mouths wide, tongues dancing, each wanting to consume the other.

They rustled and rolled, adjusting to their horizontal position but never disengaging. They jerked and struggled into comfort. He lay on top of her, his hand pushed into her hair, keeping her head from the ground, out of the dirt.

She pulled her head away, panting. "Oh! You're hot."

“No. No, you’re the hot one.” He leaned in to kiss her again.

In a moment, she pulled away once more. “No, I mean you’re on fire!” she said in a new, firm tone.

“No, you’re the one–” he managed to say before she hit him hard on the back, slapping at him as fast as she could manage. He opened his eyes and felt the heat on his back.

IGLOOS

Alaska's moon is a headlight from heaven tonight. All the stars are arranged perfectly, distributed evenly across the sky. One of those nights, chill winter creeping up your spine for the first time. Diluting summer memories, a moment alive. You can touch someone and feel like you're really holding on; you talk, and it sounds like something is being said.

Our plastic masks removed, we can escape these awkward shells and drift endlessly over the icy ocean waves. Our secret names revealed, we talk without tongues in words unstrained by mental filters. This is where we should be forever.

But so much time is wasted, alone under this moon, the door to all our dreams. I am unable to make the astral step myself.

Nothing feels real but the memories and the knowledge of another day wasted.

I stare at the moon, hoping you're watching it too. I try to reach you, casting homing thoughts into the cold air. I'm hoping you'll meet me halfway, your empty gaze colliding with mine, somewhere between us, underneath the moon.

TREE HOUSE & THE GRAVID MOON

It was late when I made it to the sledding hill. I didn't have to worry much about traffic spotting me as I went up toward the tree house. Hardly any cars passed this way at this hour. The night was quiet and still, with only the dull chatter of cricket conversation to keep me from being utterly alone with my thoughts.

From the top of the hill I saw a pair of dim headlights roll into view over the horizon. I snuck behind the base of the tree and gave the car a good few minutes to pass. Once I saw the red dots of taillights disappear on the opposite edge of my view, I prepared to ascend.

I sat down in the wooden saddle, tied myself in and began cranking the pulley.

I looked upward, but the clouds were low enough to completely obscure any sign of the tree fort. I was glad for the saddle and pulley. In recent years the tree's unexpected and misunderstood growth spurt had put our fort well over six stories up, much too high for any of us to climb.

Once I started making my way up, the cranking became a less strenuous task. The buzz of bugs and electric lights slipped away. For a moment my soul was completely disconnected, alone in this moment between the Earth below and the tree house above. Little charges of pink and purple light spattered my vision, my eyes trying to adjust to the utter empty black all around me. I sucked in nearly frozen mists; the cold air cut between my teeth and made my gums throb.

I finally broke through the blanket of clouds and saw the incredible moon. I tried to breathe right, but my throat seemed unable to take in any more frozen air. I calmed myself as best I could, and looking up I saw the tree house almost in reach now. The great red full moon bounced light off the top of the clouds, searing their edges orange and brown.

I ascended into the fort and saw someone sleeping in the far corner. It was Hercule, one of the newer members of our circle. He snored something terrible, a rhythmic growl like a lawn mower that won't start no matter how many times you yank the pull cord.

The inside of the tree house was permeated with the sickly sweet stench of stale beer, and I could make out the hint of empty bottles in the dark corner by Hercule's head.

I unfastened myself from the saddle and moved inside the tree house. In the darkness, my foot knocked into something, a sharp clink of glass. The kicked bottle crashed loudly into a few more. Clattering, they toppled over.

Hercule reflexively jumped at the sound of the bottles smacking each other. He let out a sound: part growl, part groan and part sigh. He staggered into a sitting position.

"Hey, what's up, man?" An extra-large yawn stretched the limits of his mouth.

"Not much, not much. Sorry I woke you."

"Naw, it's alright." He had returned to his original upright position. His legs crossed under him on the floor, and the back of his head was leaning against the wood wall. "I was just sleeping off a little buzz."

"How long have you been up here?"

Hercule's eyes danced around the room, looking for a clock or a way to tell time from a beer bottle, or perhaps by the number of them. "Not sure. What time is it?"

"I'm not sure either." I shook my head. "It's either really early or extremely late."

"What year is this?" He actually looked concerned, but I couldn't tell absolutely. The slight hint of a sly smile betrayed my belief that he was being earnest. I didn't know his sense of humor yet.

I snickered but didn't reply.

"Where's that girl of yours?" he asked. "The one you're always with, the one they call your bodyguard."

"She's putting in a few hours at the pizza place. She'll be by later with some food."

Hercule gave a satisfied grunt. He glanced up toward the window in the east wall as semi-warm bolts of hazy red moonlight smeared over the glass.

"Is it morning? What is that?" He got to his feet after a few fumbles and false starts.

"Check out the moon tonight," I said. "Huge, round and glowing red."

He leaned against the window, squinting at the moonlight coming in, thawing his face. He touched the glass, curled a finger around a beam of the warm light. A soft, content sound was allowed to pour from the back of his throat and bounce off the glass.

"Isn't that something? I wish I could remember the word for that kind of moon."

Hercule spun his head to look directly at me, seeming more focused than a few moments ago. "Full." He regarded me with an odd, unreadable expression. "It's called a full moon."

"No, I mean the color." I tried to keep any hint of frustration out of my voice. "There is a word for a big, red moon like that."

"Why do they need a new word?" He slowly traced random shapes on the window. "Why can't they just call it red?"

"Gravid," I said, once the word had finally broken out of its cage in the lower sections of my brain.

Hercule shrugged. "I don't care. I think it would be better if we could just blow up the moon and be done with it."

I took a few moments before I spoke, giving the words ample time to register in my head, making sure I was really hearing what he was saying. "Why would we want to blow up the moon?"

"Couple reasons." He seemed far away as he explained. "I saw a movie where aliens are coming to invade Earth. So to set up a base camp as close to us as they could, they huddled together on the dark side of the moon and made plans for their attack."

He looked at me, seemingly expecting a reaction. I had no words.

"Also werewolves," he continued. "Without a full moon, no one would ever turn into a werewolf again."

"I guess." I wasn't sure if he was joking or serious about this idea of blowing up the moon. I wasn't certain about the proper way to respond, so I gave up the least information I could but encouraged him to say more.

"Like in that Star Wars movie where the planet they live on has two moons." Hercule sounded especially grave as he approached this portion of his thoughts. "Do you think it means they have twice as many werewolves, or maybe they're just twice as strong? Maybe it means that they have twice as many werewolf nights. And what happens if both moons are full at the same time?"

"You don't really believe in werewolves and aliens, do you?"

He shot me a long, disapproving glance. "You're one of those science and logic guys, aren't you? But you can't prove werewolves don't exist."

"Well, that's true," I conceded. "Science could never prove one hundred percent beyond a doubt that something doesn't exist, even aliens and werewolves and the Loch Ness Monster."

"But if I showed you a werewolf," Hercule said, carefully weighing each word to add gravity to the point he was trying to make, "that would prove they did exist, right? So believing something could be true and could be proven right is more logical than believing something is not true even though you will never be able to absolutely prove it. So I'm ahead in the game."

"I guess." My mind reeled to find the loophole in his circular logic, or maybe it was a noose, a trap intentionally laid out for me. "Still, the moon does so much for us. It regulates the tides, and millions of animals rely on it for mating and migratory cues. Blowing it up as werewolf prevention seems to be throwing the baby out with the bath water."

"What's that mean?" He squinted at me. "Throwing the baby out with the bath water?"

"It's just an expression." I tried to find an easy way to describe it. "Going overboard, I think. Like cutting off your own head to spite your nose."

"Anyone ever tell you you talk funny?" Hercule's voice was serious, but he kept a smile on his face to let the conversation remain light. "Sometimes I can't understand a word you say. I thought you meant to say that babies can't breathe underwater."

A spurt of laughter choked out of me. "Well, that too, I guess."

Hercule turned and gave me a long, grave stare. I knew I had upset him with my last remark, but I wasn't sure how. Before he spoke again, he drove home his point by spitting onto the wooden floor of the tree house. "Guys like you think you've got everything figured out and know everything about everything. And think nothing of it, laughing at people like me and telling us what we can and cannot do."

I stammered a moment, not entirely sure what I was being accused of. "Well, people really can't breathe underwater. I didn't mean any offense by it."

"No, it's just the way you automatically assume you know better." I could hear in his voice that I had really ruffled some feathers. "You think everything you know is automatically right."

I looked up at him and met his gaze, but I didn't say a word. I still wasn't really sure what he was getting at.

"It's true, you or I, we couldn't breathe underwater." His mood calmed a little as he explained. He knelt down next to where the beer bottles were gathered and scattered, tipping a few with careful fingers. He came to one that had remained standing and looked to be nearly half full. "We would drown, no doubt. But a baby, if you trained him from a real young age, kept him in an aquarium some of the time, he would adapt. He would learn to breathe underwater and would still be able to do it as an adult."

He pulled the bottle closer, feeling the side of it with his other hand. "It's almost cold still." With no further hesitation he put the beer to his lips and drained its remaining contents.

I had been weighing my response carefully. I really didn't want to upset him any further, but there was that nagging part in my brain that just couldn't let him believe something so wrong. "It's just not possible, man. People don't have gills."

"Gills!" he scoffed. "What the hell are gills? Lungs for breathing underwater. We already got lungs, so we're halfway there."

Hercule held the empty bottle by the neck, letting it rock in his delicate grip. He was looking up through the gap between the top of the wooden walls and the roof, a full eighteen inches or so higher. He cocked the bottle quickly over his shoulder and flung it out through the space in the top of the tree fort.

I couldn't hold my tongue now. "Dammit, man, you shouldn't have done that! That was stupid!"

He spat on the floor again. "You can't tell me what I should or shouldn't do. You're not the boss of this place. I have just as much right to be here as you. You sure as hell can't tell me I can't raise an aquarium baby to breathe under goddamn water! If you knew anything, you'd know what it says in the Bible. And I've known since Sunday School that the Jonas Brothers lived for three days inside a whale. Three days! Now how the hell could they do that without no gills?"

I was stumped. I was unable to react. It wasn't a seamless, logically impenetrable defense, but more a statement so flawed and hastily constructed, so fragile – ready to crumble at the slightest breeze or doubt – that it was impossible to get a mental grip on it without the whole thing folding in on itself.

In the distance, in the night, glass crashed and broke. It seemed like an impossible amount of time since Hercule had thrown the bottle that I had all but forgotten about it.

He giggled to himself.

"I didn't come up here to pick a fight," I tried to explain matter-of-factly. I felt drained and defeated. "The whole reason I come up here is to get away from the craziness down there. I can't tell you what to do. I just didn't want to draw any unneeded attention to the fort."

"Aw, don't worry, no one's going to find us up here. They'll never see us." Hercule plucked the next least-empty and closest-to-coldest bottle from the pile, poured it down his throat and ejected it through the space above the wall. He burped and smiled as widely as I'd ever seen. "You just sit and relax and wait for your girl with your pizza."

He leaned his head back and looked out at nothing in particular. But he was certainly giving the impression he was done with the conversation.

We sat there in silence for a few moments until we heard a second crash of glass out below, followed by a quick screech of tires. This made Hercule laugh once again, harder now and repeating, but still to himself.

I leaned my own head back and stared up at nothing. I shut my eyes and tried to close my mind off from the world. I had a terrible feeling it was going to be a long, strange night.

STREETS TURNED UGLY

Wandering back onto streets I haven't walked in years. Who was it who used to talk about the streets as if they were ours, as if we owned them? 'These are our streets!'

Somehow we have lost our title or lost control, or maybe we walked away in disgust.

Now the reflections that peek back from dirty windows come across as unfamiliar and awkward. I can imagine myself in this same spot seven years ago, looking into shop windows as I pass, catching reflections of ghosts staring back at me.

Only now I realize I was seeing pictures of myself from the future, how I look now.

These mirrors don't recognize me anymore. No longer can they compliment me. I stare at myself and feel at odds, as if I should think of something to say. But I can't; it feels useless and trite.

I stand alone, trying to find a few words to offer myself. I only stare back, speechless, hollow and afraid, no longer able to face me.

WORLD INTERVENTION WEEK

With the deadline fast approaching, Elvis Grubecheck was beyond stressed. Ten televisions whipped ten separate images at him, all in double speed. The high-pitched soundtrack, like overlapped chipmunk conversations, filled the room and Elvis' mind, making him more frantic.

Assistants and staff lurked and scurried in the shadows, the phones on his desk rang and beeped, and even his computer flashed with a half dozen imminent matters, over each of which he held a distinct and individual sense of dread. And all of this before lunch.

He rang down to the receptionist. "Mr. Grubecheck," she began as soon as she picked up the call, "please tell me that I can send these guys from the Local Business Interest in. They've been in here almost an hour, sir." Lowering her voice to a whisper, the receptionist then added, "Frankly, they're starting to stink up the showroom."

"Rosa, have you seen the lunch guy?" Elvis asked her, stressing each word to instill the importance he placed on eating right now.

"Oh, yeah, he's on his way up," she replied, aloof and contemptuous. "I was just thinking that since you're seeing people now, you might pick up one of these phones that have been waiting so patiently for you to answer them."

There was a knock at the door. Elvis pressed a button, and the door opened slightly. The lunch guy pushed his way quietly into the noisy office.

Rosa the receptionist's voice still cut through the din of electronic media and alarms, a finely honed inflection and pitch specifically trained for this purpose, and piped into Elvis' office over the intercom: "This lawyer from Pepsi has been trying to reach you since this morning. He's called six times, after waiting as long as he possibly could each time. And then there are the people from MTV. They are very insistent that they speak to you before we air. I was just thinking that since you're taking a break—"

"I'm eating," Elvis interrupted her as soon as he found a chance, waving the delivery boy over to his desk. "Tell them all to call back in an hour."

He tapped the button on the desk, disconnecting his office from her, and regarded the kid in the red and blue delivery jacket with a paper bag in his arm, who was gazing about the office in utter awe, completely overwhelmed.

"I've never been in a television studio before," the lunch guy said once he realized he had Mr. Grubecheck's attention. "This is all pretty cool."

"This is hell, kid," Elvis replied, deadpan. "How much do I owe you?"

"Hell?" The lunch guy cracked a surprised smile and dropped the bag of food into Elvis' expectant hands. "I couldn't help overhearing your secretary, and you get to talk to people from Pepsi and MTV! I can't imagine that's hell."

"First of all, she's not my secretary. She works for the station, and she hates me," Elvis said as he reached into his back pocket for his wallet. He felt no obligation to explain matters to the kid, but he was simply exhausted, overworked and isolated, in need of some verbal release, even if it was only venting the desperation of his situation to a restaurant delivery boy. "Second of all, the guy from Pepsi is a lawyer. It seems one of the local trees we were going to feature was near a garbage can, and in the background of the scene you can see a discarded Pepsi can on the ground. And if that can is seen on the air tonight in the course of our programming, Pepsi is going to sue me for millions.

"As for the guys from MTV," Elvis continued, not noticing that his stressed and angry gaze was unnerving the boy or that the more he ranted, the more scared the boy became, "we have an hour-long interview with a scientist from the local arboretum. It was shot in front of a rare *Bois Dentelle* tree, of which there are only two known to exist. That particular tree has an abnormal knot that at a certain angle resembles the MTV logo, and they are quite adamant that if I want to show that interview in front of a *Bois Dentelle*, I'd better find another one."

Elvis stood silent for a minute, finally seeing the glazed-over look on the lunch guy's face, who was unsure of how or if he should react.

"Man, I never wanted any of this," Elvis said resignedly as he plopped himself down in the large control chair. "All I wanted was to save a few of the trees on my block and in the neighborhood. A few of us got together and started a community ecology club, just trying to raise awareness, really, and maybe save a few of this town's quickly vanishing trees while we were at it. We've had over fifty species that used to be predominant in these hills completely disappear from this state in the last twenty years. Did you know that?"

The boy shook his head.

"Anyway," Elvis continued, waving his arm in the air for emphasis, "somehow as we got bigger, we got involved with this big nationwide ecological-political front. Honestly, they flashed a lot of cash around, and we were taken. They promised us national exposure and lobby power in Congress. We had our day in court, and somehow when all the smoke cleared, our town was left with this." Elvis waved at the television equipment around him, still talking away to itself and beeping and whirring.

The delivery guy looked around for a few seconds and then carefully started, "Well, television is a great–"

"They're still cutting down our trees!" Elvis shouted, banging an open palm against his desk. "All we wanted was to protect a couple trees, and instead we have a court-mandated week of television overriding all the local networks once a year. It's called World Intervention Week, and it's our time to teach the town about environmentalism. For one full week a year, one hundred seventy-two hours of quality ecology television programming, whether you like it or not. We're on every station."

"Well, okay," the delivery guy conceded. "I can see how that might not–"

"I walked out of here last year - after a week of trees, and tree talk, and movies with trees in them, and more interviews with trees - and have had my life threatened every damn day since. 'I better not have to sit through another week of tree TV. I know where you live!'"

Elvis was visibly shaken and sweating now. He wiped at his head with a sleeve and tried to control his breathing. He was nearly hyperventilating.

The lunch delivery guy reached into his coat and pulled out a pack of cigarettes. He wrapped his lips around a smoke and pulled it from the pack, then offered the pack to Elvis. "What if I told you I could make it all go away?"

Elvis accepted a cigarette and paused. Eager for a solution, but also very skeptical, he asked, "What do you mean?"

"I can change the past," the delivery guy stated as a matter of fact, lighting his smoke and taking in a long drag. "I can redirect certain situations in history to make it so that you never got tied up in this mess."

"I'm up to my neck in shit as it is. I do not need for you to come in here and insult my intelligence–"

"Not at all," the delivery guy interrupted with a wave of his hand. "I can prove it. I completely abide by the Pennsylvania State Time Continuum Code."

Elvis retorted in disgust, "That's a stupid piece of bureaucratic red tape that likens Daylight Saving Time to witchcraft or sorcery."

"I am speaking of the second part of the Code," the lunch boy continued, calm and poised now, "what they aptly call the *Philip K. Dick* clause: Any claims of being able to either travel in time or change past occurrences must, to be legitimately verified, be challenged to the death. Only in this extreme trial can the validity of the claim be completely proven or denied. If the person making the claim allows himself to be killed, then he was surely bluffing and thus was unable to affect time to even save himself. If he remains alive, he is telling the truth and has the ability to alter the past. In any other attempt to demonstrate such phenomenal abilities, the claimant will be unable to completely convince anyone, and any spectator will be unable to be completely free of doubt."

Elvis eyed the kid, letting lazy smoke rings fall from his mouth and climb up his face. He wondered if he had snapped, if he was having some sort of psychotic hallucination, or if this was really happening. Was this delivery boy really saying what he seemed to be saying, about to challenge Elvis to try to kill him?

"Before I came in to your office," the lunch guy continued, "I placed a 9 mm handgun in the little vestibule out in the hall. I knew where the sequence of events was headed. I knew you would confess some dire situation to me and that I would tell you of my gift. And I knew you would not believe me. So being someone who believes in the law–"

"That is not a law," Elvis muttered, getting up from behind his desk and heading toward the door. "It is a license to shoot crazy people."

He went out of the office and directly toward the little vestibule opposite the doorway. He wondered how a person snaps like that, wakes up one day with the delusion that he can alter time, a delusion for which he is willing to die.

Opening the little drawer at the top, Elvis found the gun. As soon as he touched it, a jolt of adrenaline shot up his spine. Gripping its weight in his hands, he felt an odd power. *I am going to kill that crazy bastard*. The thought filled his head with an ugly sense of satisfaction. *It may be the only release I get to feel today.*

Barging back into the office, Elvis challenged the lunch guy, "Why don't you go back in time and make it so trees never existed?"

"I could," the kid offered calmly, "but the really sad part would be that you would never know they existed in the first place. You wouldn't even know to miss them."

Elvis sat back down, aiming the gun across the desk at the delivery boy but finding it impossible to steady his arm now. "I don't know what kind of sick you are," he started on the boy, "but you really picked the wrong day to go crazy and come in here and unleash it on me. I have to be on the air in less than three hours, and you come in here and insult my intelligence and eat up my time with this load of nonsense? Well, I'm not sorry for what I'm about to do. You've brought it on yourself."

Elvis pulled the tab back, and the contents of the soda can spat and fizzled out, splashing his face and wetting his desk. He tossed the still-overflowing can into the wastebasket by the side of his desk and went searching for paper towels. A strange chill swept through his body for a moment.

"Are you convinced, then?" the delivery boy asked.

Elvis stopped. "Are you still on that nonsense?" he demanded.

"Why did you just get up and leave your office a minute ago?"

"I told you, I was thirsty. I asked if you wanted a drink," Elvis said, but then he remembered going to the vestibule and grabbing a soda. And as he touched the can, he recalled that for an instant he was sure he was going to walk back into his office and kill the lunch guy with it. He shook his head in an attempt to make his thoughts fall in the proper order in his brain, and then sat himself back down behind his desk.

The lunch guy still sat there, looking expectantly at Elvis. So Elvis reflexively reached into his wallet to pay him. He handed him the cash and said, "Look, whatever you are offering, I don't want any part of it. I don't care if it is real or not. I am incredibly busy here, and I need to be left alone."

"No tip, then?" the delivery guy asked, counting the cash.

"Just get out," Elvis said, not looking at him, trying to dive back into the mess around him: the week-long television program he was legally bound to produce, the unending phone calls and alarms, the rat race of compiling a week's worth of footage and all the technical difficulties related to it.

As the door closed behind the delivery guy, Elvis Grubecheck felt cold air rush for an instant against his face, and with it, a fleeting memory of some nostalgic scent that he couldn't place in his mind. Like *deja vu*, it left him out of sorts for a second.

He began flipping through his production notes to reconnect his mind to the work ahead of him. As he read, he came across a huge matter that had somehow eluded him to this point. Occurring in almost every aspect of the show was this word, this item, that Elvis could not identify. It appeared to play a pivotal part in the television program he was about to produce, but he had no idea for the life of him what it was.

He rang down to the receptionist. "Rosa, what the hell is a tree?"

"Never heard of it Mr. Grubecheck," she replied in her condescending manner. "Now if you want to talk about the people here waiting to see you–"

"T. R. E. E." He spelled it out to her, this word that was riddled throughout his notes.

"Would you like me to ask the people waiting to talk to you if they have ever heard of this tree thing?" She raised her voice at him now.

"Yes," he snapped, "do that." And he disconnected the call.

Somehow he doubted that any of them would.

Elvis stood up from his desk and went over to his office window. *Something has happened here today,* he thought, although he could not for the life of him figure out what. Something to do with that crazy delivery guy. *I better make sure we don't order from there again.*

He gripped his production notes, a two-thousand-page document that he had just realized was mostly meaningless to him. *How am I going to produce a week-long uninterrupted show about something that neither I nor anyone else has ever heard of?* His heart skipped a panicked beat. How could he miss something so glaring until now, when he was only two hours to showtime?

He peered out his window, past the buildings of his small city, past the brown sand of the surrounding hills, and off toward the flat yellow and gold deserts of North America. He wondered what to do, who to call. Something in his bones told him that he could look for years and never find a human being who had ever heard of this thing, the tree.

THE LYING DOG SLEEPS

You wake me at this hour because the dog barked. The dog barked once and seemed to be looking toward the door. You saw no light, no sign of movement, and heard no noise, but you want me to check if there is anyone outside.

You do not know my dog very well. If she is barking at night, it means there might be a rabbit in the yard. Granted, it always seems to be the same rabbit, and yes, it does seem to be taunting the dog. The rabbit will sit in the yard, perfectly still, seeming to stare sidelong at the dog. Plus, I have never before seen a rabbit that can smirk.

Fireworks and rainstorms also freak her out – luckily, the fireworks are limited to certain holidays, sporting events, general elections, visits from the Easter Bunny, tooth faerie or Santa Klaus, a kid's good report card, a family celebration or event or commemoration or dinner together, an especially good rerun of *The Simpsons*, or just to break up the general monotony of people being able to sleep at night.

And the storm has to be pretty severe, or at least highlighted with thunder or lightning, or be a heavy, noisy splattering of water on the roof, or sometimes a light drizzle will do it, or if the weatherman accidentally says the word *rain*, or if someone down the block happens to be running a bath.

If I opened the door and saw a person standing there, staring in, it would probably shake me out of my shoes. But the dog, I don't think she would be afraid or get nervous. Not if there was any slim chance that this stranger might scratch her belly or offer a bit of food.

UNSEEN ARCHITECT

At first I didn't notice it at all. Strange that I could miss something so large and unexpected. But they say even the Natives living in America didn't notice the Spanish ships approaching until they were already upon them because there was nothing in their experience or memory to explain such a sight, no point of reference.

I stepped out my back door with my cup of coffee held close to my face for warmth and for the small bit of caffeine that might creep into my system by osmosis until the coffee cooled enough to let me take a proper drink. I lit my morning cigarette and exhaled a cloud of smoke into the foggy air.

After a few small sips of coffee and a few drags from my smoke, I was nearly ready to make my way back into the house and get on with my day when I caught a slight idea that something was not right. Something was askew in the yard.

I nearly jumped right out of my slippers when I finally allowed myself to see the swimming pool taking up most of my backyard. A swimming pool that had not been there the night before. I didn't order a swimming pool, and I was not expecting one.

And, let me be clear here, it was not just a hole dug into the ground and filled with water. This was a completely constructed and finished pool. Long, straight edges where the water met a concrete walkway. A railing around the perimeter to keep the area safe and not trampled upon by unexpected wandering neighborhood children. A beautiful, gleaming tiled patio area with a few tables set up and umbrellas for shade, and a row of reclining deck chairs for catching some sun. A few plastic inflatables bobbing up and down in the water, and at the far end, a diving board over the edge of the pool, looking professionally installed and solid.

My mouth opened and closed a few times without any indication of whether it meant to say something or was trying to get more oxygen to my brain.

I was completely dumbfounded.

Had aliens landed in my backyard and, finding no animals to mutilate or reclusive drunkards to abduct, decided instead to blow my mind and install a swimming pool? This was as plausible as any other explanation as I could fathom at the moment.

I wanted to ask someone, call someone. Where could I even go to find out what had happened? My immediate thought was to call the police. But what would I say? I'm reporting a swimming pool being installed in my yard overnight without my permission?

I thought if they didn't send a patrol car over, I could certainly expect a visit from a psychiatrist or some state mental health advisory board member.

Maybe I could ask a neighbor. But even this task would have to be handled delicately, or I would forever lose my standing in the community and be labeled as the 'crazy swimming pool guy'.

Perhaps I should just try to play it off as normal. I had intended to have a pool installed, and I just forgot about making the plans final, or I had ordered it late one night on eBay after too many drinks.

I heard some stirring from next door, the screen door being pulled aside and my neighbor coming out to her yard for her similar morning ritual of coffee and a cigarette.

Almost immediately she let out a loud screech, and I heard a crash. Her ceramic coffee mug shattered on the concrete.

I made my way to the fence and peered over into her yard. Apparently she hadn't taken so long to notice the same thing: a swimming pool where none had been the day before, looking exactly like mine.

I called out to her, "You too, huh?"

She met my gaze but was unable to focus, a lost, scared look on her face. Her eyes were red from sleep and shock. It took her a few moments to formulate any words. "Do you know about this?"

"No, ma'am," I tried to console her, or at least assure her that I was as clueless as she. "I just got up and saw the same thing in my yard. No idea, no explanation. I thought maybe I ordered it in a blackout, until I saw yours."

She gazed over the fence and saw my pool. She looked out over the neighborhood, reached out her arm and waved, trying to point in every direction at once. She apparently had noticed something I hadn't.

"Look at them!" She was nearly crying now. "Look at all of them!"

I looked out over the whole neighborhood, and my stomach turned in fear and incomprehension. Every house on the block, most likely every yard in the subdivision, was now fitted with an identical swimming pool, unwanted and unexpected.

We stared for a few silent minutes. The last drops of coffee splattered out of my cup, as I could no longer keep my hand steady.

It seemed doubly sinister. A swimming pool in itself is not an ominous sight. Very few horror movies use a swimming pool as a scary motif, unless of course there is a shark or an electric eel or displaced corpses from where the yard used to be a cemetery.

But this was so unusual, it made it that much more frightening. If someone broke into my garage and stole my car, or spray-painted slurs and epithets on the side of my house, I would feel wronged and dirty, but at least it would be explainable, understandable.

My neighbor opened the gate and let herself into my yard without a word. She approached me and collapsed against me, and I put my arms around her. I tried to comfort her as best I could, though I could find little comfort myself.

I had been violated. I had been intruded upon, as had the whole community. And I wasn't even sure where to start looking, or who to ask without putting my sanity into question.

I forgot the notion of going to work that morning. I forgot entirely about the hundreds of little Post-it notes in my mind marked 'urgent' and 'things to do today'. This was much more important than any of that, much more pressing. It was vital that I figure it out, this inexplicable act of aggression by some unseen architect or a crew of roaming carpenters and landscapers.

I had no idea how, or where to go to seek answers. Our lives were tipped over, in an instant turned upside down. My world took a definite turn toward strange, and I had a feeling it would only grow stranger.

DRUNK DIALING

HERMETIC LABORATORIES ANNOUNCED today that it has developed a new application for smartphones called iBlow and plans to offer it to the retail market in early spring.

The iBlow app works much the same as the Breathalyzers used in the field by law enforcement. The user exhales into the smartphone's mouthpiece, where the breath is digitally analyzed to determine the user's blood-alcohol content.

From there, the way the phone reacts is completely customizable, with different BAC levels and contact lists.

For instance, users can set their phones so that calling friends after one or two beers would be permitted, but calls would be disconnected or prohibited after a twelve-pack of malt liquor.

Also, users will be able to configure iBlow so after a night of heavy drinking, they would be able to call for a pizza, but all of their ex-girlfriends/boyfriends would be blocked.

Hermetic Labs hopes iBlow will be a helpful and popular application, and starting in April it will be available wherever liquor and cell phones are sold.

The company also expects to release similar apps for eBay, to eliminate '*buzzed buying*' and '*blackout shopping sprees*', as well as for social networking sites such as Facebook and Twitter. Myspace, however, will still require a seven-drink minimum.

GARAGE DOOR REVISTED

Fezby handed me the keys, a pointed tangle of metal poking my hand, digging into my skin.

"You'll have to drive. You'll have to do it somehow," he stuttered, trying to talk without getting enough air in his lungs. "I can't. Look at me - okay, sorry I said that. But I can't drive, trust me. I'll guide you, be your eyes."

I followed his footsteps, and I could tell he wasn't walking right either. One foot struck the ground hard, and the other dragged after it.

I heard the chime of the open door and felt my way into the driver's seat. Fezby shut me in and made his way around to the other side.

I sat for a moment, the clump of keys in my hand, unsure what I was supposed to do next.

"Here," Fezby said, trying to guide my hand. I didn't know what he was trying to make me do, and I felt I was fighting him, getting in his way. He took the keys from me and put them wherever they needed to go.

The engine fired up, and the car purred around me. I could hardly believe I was expected to operate this heavy machine. The rattling, vibrating pulse under my legs and up my back was the car letting me know it waited on my word.

Fezby grabbed my hand, guiding it to a cold and somewhat sticky sort of handle. I studied it, working my grip around it. The top was scalloped to fit my fingers.

"This is the gearshift." Fezby's hand over mine nudged my thumb to depress a button, and the handle felt free to move in my grip. "The steering wheel is in front of you. And at your feet are the pedals; these are important: the gas is on your right, and the brake is on the left. Step on the brake, and I'll put us in gear."

I kicked around with my feet. They became entangled with two protrusions. I couldn't get a good feel of them, rushed by Fezby's urgency. I stepped on the left, and the pedal moved against the pressure.

Fezby yanked my hand, and the plastic handle moved back, clicking past a few notches. The car came to life under me, around me, vibrating harder and louder, responding to me.

"You're going to take your foot off the brake, and the car will move backwards. When I say stop, press the brake; when I say go faster, press the gas pedal on the right. When I tell you to turn, just twist the steering wheel in front of you." Fezby's voice calmed a little. "I'm sorry. I know you don't want to do this, and I don't want to ride with you, no offense. But I don't see we have much choice. Let go of the brake and back us out."

I let pressure off my leg and felt the pedal releasing. I thought it was stuck to my shoe the way it leaned in on my foot. The car bucked under me. My stomach dropped as far down into my intestines as it could manage. I was thrown for a moment from my seat, and the car growled loudly at me. I heard a crashing, a grinding of metal, a buckling or crunching. My head hit something in front of me, the windshield, and I heard Fezby hit it too. He cried out in surprise or pain or both. The car still purred, agitated now but not moving. I had made it mad or bristled its fur or something.

"What did I do?" My forehead throbbed where my head had hit against the glass, the pain piercing my skull. My left hand gripped the steering wheel. I wasn't sure if I was shaking that hard or if the car was shaking me.

"I put us in the wrong gear." Fezby's excited tone calmed enough to let a slight laugh break through. "You hit the garage door. Bent it right in.

Don’t worry, I’ll fix that later. This is going to be harder than I thought.”

That didn’t exactly ease my fear, my nerves, the awful feeling of having no idea what I was doing. But Fezby was right, he couldn’t drive. I was going to have to do the best I could with his direction and hope I didn’t kill us or anyone else on the way.

We hadn’t moved much at all, and I’d crashed into the garage. It didn’t make me feel comfortable or in control. I was afraid if we actually did make it to the hospital, both of us would be in need of medical attention.

HUMANS

I thought I was in love, but it was only a head cold. I've been awake for three days with my skin feeling like it's dried out and constricting against my bones.

I sometimes forget that I'm not a turtle anymore. I try to retract into my shell but end up making a genetic mess of myself.

Standing somewhere looking incredibly stupid and uncool, I suddenly realize where I am and who I am: it's sometime in the last part of the twentieth century, and I am one of those goofy Humans that seem to be all the fashion these days.

I spend much of my time at the end of a counter taking coffee and conversation with a number of different humans, many of them miserable.

The girl who sits at the other end of the counter, blowing long, graven rings of cigarette smoke over her coffee, is spinning her latest tale of woe: "My car broke down, and as I stepped out it blew up, destroying my *Precious Sledd* CD collection. All my hair burnt off and I went to work anyway, but the place was just gone!

"Poof! No trace, just an empty office. I asked a few of the building maintenance people, but none of them had ever heard of the company I worked for or recognized me. They said the office suite I was talking about had been vacant as long as any of them could remember.

"I knew there was something fishy about it the whole time, but I still can't really put a finger on it." She shrugs, an admittance and acceptance of defeat and failure. "Oh well, sucks to be me."

"I was you for five days," I say to her, "and it happened to be the best week of my life."

She gives me the lunatic smile I've grown so accustomed to seeing. "What are you talking about? Being me?"

"It was that week a few years ago that you can't remember. You had that accident on your ski vacation in Zurich and found yourself a week later wandering along the edge of the Nile."

Her face turns white, and she gasps. "Oh my God! That's right! I had blocked the whole thing from memory. I can't believe I projected all my insecurities and fears onto my cat, Vishnu. I've been taking him to pet psychiatrists for years! Oh my, it's all coming back to me now." She shakes her head quickly and smiles.

I wait until her eyes meet mine and continue, "Now, do you remember this? Way back, many, many years ago, before cars, before electricity, before even money, you were called Otuugluu and lived in the cave closest to the water. And one morning the thin, tri-cloptic beings emerged, walking out of the ocean and onto the land. After first becoming friends, they adapted your customs. Eventually they completely blended, indiscernible from the normal folks. Until one day–"

I was interrupted by the arrival of her bus. She said she wanted to hear how it turned out, but for now, she really had to leave.

Of course, I never saw her again. Soon after, someone in Los Angeles decided to surgically attach himself to his car and was no longer able to go anywhere that didn't have a drive-through window.

Within a few weeks it was the newest trend in America. By the time the decade closed out, anyone who was anybody had been stitched permanently into their cars, their internal organs synced up with the electronics and mechanics of the engine.

The '*cool*' people of the Earth, at one with their vehicles.

Everyone else was forced to rearrange the world to accommodate. Every form of business was required to install a drive-through, and the dentist's office was soon made into the dentist's garage.

All the uncouth, the losers of the world, those of us not surgically connected to our automobiles, we were all very helpful and pleasant in adapting the planet to their whim. We all found it amusing, and we chuckled silently to ourselves.

Trapped in their cars now for the duration of their lives, the trendsetters and socially superior found themselves incapable of any physical contact with any other cool person, or in fact at all.

Ultimately it meant they were unable to produce offspring.

We, the peasants, the pedestrian, those of us who were well removed from the cutting edge, we give a knowing smile as we pass the cars on the street, as we watch them convert another parking garage into condos, as we wait on them in the window of the grocery store drive-through express lane.

Quietly it echoes in the hearts of humans all over the world: 'We are finally rid of these bastards.'

HEADLONG

Many guides and teachers will spell out things you need to know to become a better writer. Everyone has a few rules they insist you must obey and quite a few skills you must learn in order to effectively execute your efforts.

Before any of these things can come into play – before spelling, grammar, style and storytelling – there's an essential step that usually goes unspoken, and indeed may not be mentioned at all in most lessons.

Learning how to become a better writer, rule number one: Put down the pen, step away from the blank page, and dive headlong into life. Get in and get messy. Invest many hours in things that will 'build character,' make as many mistakes as you can stand, and be sure to participate in scenarios you are sure to 'look back and laugh about' one day. Collect the scenes and funny asides, and get to know your characters.

Don't think of writing, don't look for stories. Just live, and let the stories unfold naturally. Some won't become apparent until much later, when they can be filtered through several years of perspective and experience.

I have spent many years training for this role, and much of the time I wasn't aware what I was really doing. Now I find there's very little I need to create or imagine. I have collected some stories I would never have believed had I not been a witness. I only have to change a few names and pixelate the faces, and the stories I am provided are far weirder and more authentic than anything I could ever think up on my own.

Teachers and writers usually suggest you 'write what you know,' and unfortunately this is the brutal truth. No matter how well you command the language, no matter your talent for capturing attention with the stories you tell, it is futile to expect anyone to read your work if it turns out you have nothing to say.

Dig in to life, and get your hands dirty. Take it all in; the good, the bad, the ugly and strange. There will be many lessons to learn, always the hard way. There will be much to observe – and yes, this will all be covered on the test.

If you do it right, you will laugh often and cry when you must; you will become completely immersed in the game. Filthy, awkward and blushing. People may well ask what the hell you think you're doing, but you will be too wrapped up inside the story to explain:

"Please excuse me. It's part of my training. I am trying to become a better writer."

ABRAHAM PRESLEY

Abraham Lincoln and Elvis Presley happen to run into one another in a barbershop. The barber is so surprised to see the both of them together that he accidentally chops off their heads and nervously tries to sew them back on but ends up switching them around.

They leave and go their separate ways without noticing the mix-up. The Abraham Lincoln body with the Elvis head makes it halfway to the park when he notices what happened. After a minute of apprehension and confusion, he becomes excited at the potential and possibilities made available by this combination of Lincoln-body and Elvis-head.

He rushes around the town performing great deeds; bounding with energy, he zips from tragedy to crisis, overjoyed by the thrill of assisting them all. He rescues a cat from a tree, saves children from a burning building, helps an elderly couple across a busy intersection and then reroutes the road to make it less crowded. He builds a library; streamlines the town's financial structure, saving the townspeople tax dollars; and clubs a group of seal clubbers.

Filled with the immense sense of accomplishment - not ego-driven, but pure joy from doing good - he walks back into town toward the barbershop to express his sincere gratitude for the serendipitous slice and swap.

On the sidewalk near the barbershop, he sees his other half - the Lincoln-headed Elvis-body - slowly shuffling along, staring at the ground. It turns its head up toward him and asks, "Where did you go off to?"

Elvis-headed Lincoln-body tells his other half of all the things he's done since discovering the change, regaling him with the good he's done. "I saved a cat from a tree and some children from a burning building, helped an elderly couple across a busy street, and then redirected traffic to ease congestion on the road. I built the town a library and restructured their finances, and I also pounded some poachers. So, please tell me," he says to his opposite self, fully anticipating some equally fulfilling stories, "what have you been doing since discovering this wonderful mishap?"

"I went to a theater," the Lincoln-head with an Elvis-body spoke meekly, grinding a shoe into gravel. "I wasted the whole day watching something called a *Three Stooges Marathon.*"

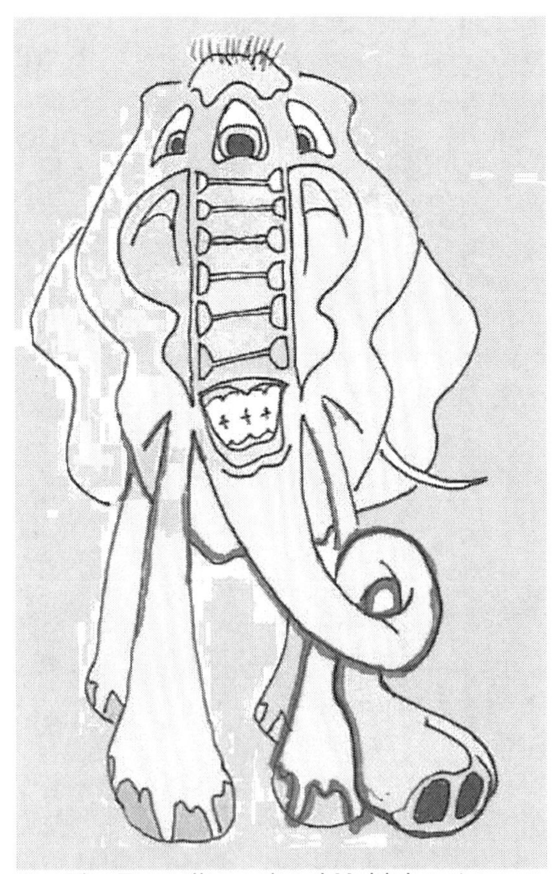

'The Transdimensional Multiphant'

THE ZIPPER

Dafne's story has always been sad. Even as successful and famous as she is now, telling her story is still a depressing endeavor.

I first met her on a hot October night in the middle of April. She was seeing Elvis Grubecheck for a time, but this was long before his tragic onset of social conscience.

The three of us sat on his porch abusing whatever trendy substances were in rotation at the time. We watched the conversation warp and wiggle the way it does only when you can't quite remember what you're talking about.

Dafne didn't talk much and mostly sat quietly, hiding behind her long black hair and Morrissey t-shirt. For a moment I wondered how long she'd worked to perfect the pout that told in one glance how much she despised life. A smothering of black mascara couldn't hide her eyes, huge and full and ready to spill over at the slightest upset.

"Ugh, I hate this," she sputtered in an urgent but pathetic voice. Neither Elvis nor I were surprised by her attitude. No one who knew her more than ten minutes would be.

"Which particular parts of this," Elvis waved his hand in the air all-inclusively, "do you hate so much? What is it specifically that you hate? And why? And please rate every item of your hatred individually on a scale of one to one hundred."

"I thought about ending it all last night." She exhaled loudly and tried to slide a tear back into her eye with a pinkie finger. This statement came as no surprise to us either.

A few months earlier, Dafne had become tired of the labor involved in slashing her wrists every time she felt like ending it. She saved up a few paychecks and had a plastic surgeon install a zipper.

Now every time she reaches that ecstatic level of misery and despair, she can easily open her wrist and let out a little blood.

She was holding her arm up now for Elvis and me to see. Covering the flesh and metal of her arm was a layer of dry black blood.

"Nobody understands, but it's okay," she whispered, her posture collapsed like an inflatable toy losing its air. She shot a quick glance at us to see if we were buying into her tantrum.

"Nope. Nobody understands," Elvis mocked her, but it was an obscure brand of sarcasm he chose to work with, and I couldn't quite recognize its root.

Dafne folded her lip over, under itself, and her eyes started overspilling like a pot of boiling water. It was utterly pathetic and unquestionably contrived. She fiddled with her zipper pull.

"That look could sell," I thought out loud. I hadn't meant to speak. But being the quick-thinking capitalist that I am, I couldn't resist the idea. All the late-night *sponsor a child* campaigns with pathetic, bug-eyed runts pleading for seventy cents a day. *Less than the price of a cup of coffee.* Dafne could give them a run for their money.

And I was right. Look at her now. She sold her misery to the world, and the world returned her soul. But even this could not make her happy.

She was in all those movies for a while, usually playing a victim of some heinous and unspeakable injustice. The public couldn't get enough, flocking by the thousands to catch a glimpse. But as much as it was her status as a star, it was equally the element in human nature that makes us slow down to catch a glance of the accident and maybe peek at bloody carnage from the seven-car pileup.

Dafne took on the misery of the world, and the world loved her for it. But even this was not enough for her.

All the Emo boys and girls started calling themselves *Zipper Bitches*, some of them going so far as to mimic and adapt Dafne's installation.

Her influence on the world struck heavy and wide, bringing us all down a little more every day. She brought out the gloom we had swept under the rug for so long, collectively putting on a good face and wanting to appear as a content and stable society.

Now people craved the darkness. And for a while the only ones willing to take the lonely way out did it purely out of spite, to add more misery to those they left behind.

Dafne looked at the world, and especially how she affected it. She had made existence increasingly miserable for all life on Earth; even the sand crabs that emerge in the full moon to mate now left tiny trails of tears on the beaches they inhabited. Even dogs and cats and caterpillars, the world was depressing and depressed.

Seeing what she had done dropped her lower into a wretched, morbid state we had never seen, more miserable than any one creature had ever managed to be. All was pain, increasing pain exponentially. Any passing thought at all now was assured to make her mood descend at least a little lower into darkness. She decided once more, one final time, to remove herself from the world.

The spectacle was televised on all networks, and a constant live stream went out to everyone tuning in or playing along at home. The *Nielsens* say it was the most-watched event in history.

An elite cast of celebrities congregated and took turns recalling terrible and heartbreaking stories, each adding a personal shade of black to the whole miserable affair, the gala magnum opus of the pessimistic life.

The evening peaked when Dafne took the stage, dressed all in black, nearly invisible but for a weak and meager spotlight, which turned out to be a badly wired garage sale lamp with duct tape wrapped around the shade.

Her face barely poked through the black. She stood posed, wilting like a trampled flower. Her expression made every facial-recognition system anywhere in the world start to doubt its own abilities and heave a sad little sigh.

The world wept along.

Dafne raised her eyes through the black mascara sandbags propping them up. She stared into the camera and whispered something none of us, no one anywhere, could hear. She then unzipped her wrist.

She waited, deflated and withering. All the blood flowed out of her. All her skin lost its color, and her face turned a sickly blue. She threw an internal, undetectable tantrum. She wondered why she was still alive, why she couldn't die.

But she was too depressed to ever die. She tried again, for as long as the networks found ways to sponsor her airtime. She shot herself, ran a steamroller over her own body, every imaginable method and quite a few no one had ever thought of.

Every unsuccessful attempt only threw her deeper into darkness and closer to realizing that the one thing that could ever make her happy was the only thing she could never have.

CLEANSING

Cleaning goes against nature. Look at your pets next time you tidy up around the house. The animals scurry away, not in fear of being swept up and discarded, but because cleaning is simply unnatural and wrong.

Everyone waved goodbye as the gym teacher ran off, struck and tumbling, in a twenty-one dodge ball salute. Cheerleaders circled, and their green and purple tongues slithered up, tangling in the high branches of the trees. The fire crackled, dancing like an Egyptian, kicking a leg out and flailing its arms to grab at those closest. Not far off a bird mimicked a song in a language not spoken for ten thousand years.

The next day, not a trace.

I was twenty-four and repeating my senior year of high school for the sixth time. But I would not give up, that's the important thing. It was hard to take it seriously anymore. The teachers were unequipped to have a student around the school for ten years, especially the teachers over whom he had tenure.

It was a precarious ledge for a young alchemist. I remember the only time I had a tarot card reading: the lady looked me straight in the eye and said, "You are a joke - the fact that you believe what you feed yourself is more frightening than it is unfathomable. I doubt you will be able to decipher what I say to you right now."

I have never had the desire to seek a reading since, and I still cannot make out the cryptic message of that strange old card-reading lady.

I went back to the woods a few times a week for the next year or so. Looking for clues, something left behind. Maybe a call from that damn bird.

It became harder to remember exactly where it all took place. I would sit on a branch and wait for the sun to set, trying to superimpose the memory on top of my surroundings to see if I was in the right spot. A couple of times, I could see the fire again.

For a moment I could watch it dancing on the rocks and feel its hand reaching out to grab me. A flash of heat against my face, and it vanished. I would sit for a minute more and then wander back to the path, noticing always a strange silence in the woods, as if the animals had all run away.

SUBROUTINE

Challenged by the inexplicably small tip left for her, the waitress turned into a seven-headed fire-breathing serpent and torched the party of cheapskates to a blackened crisp.

At the next table, a clammy-skinned, long-haired kid sat talking to a truck driver. The hippie-looking guy's muscles twitched nervously to keep the thin layer of protoplasm covering his skin from hardening into a yellow crusty shell.

He was telling the truck driver that he followed a band called *Blue Nun and The Bad Habits*. He traveled around the world catching their concerts, and he had seen them on every continent but one.

"One day," he said as a far-off gaze broke through the flimsy mucus covering his skin, "one day, I'm going to save up my money and head for Australia."

The waitress slithered over to their table, her body almost completely transformed back to human, except for her twelve-foot-long tongue, which she wrapped around the young guy's leg.

"Australia," she purred, slithering her tongue up under his shirt. "It's hot there, isn't it?"

The hippie looked up, vaguely toward the waitress, unsure how he should react. "Yeah, I guess it would be."

"Hey, can I get some more coffee?" the truck driver interrupted, a hint of jealousy seeping out of the mane of mustard-stained facial hair that seemed to be his mouth.

The waitress shot a piercing glance at the trucker and was about to annihilate him in a fury of demonic rage when she noticed his eyes, his ice-blue eyes poking out of dark, deep-rooted canyons of stress and speed, eyes that had seen an endless succession of highways and coffee mugs, hiding rigidly under one fierce, black eyebrow.

"What'cha hauling, big boy?" The waitress coyly unraveled her serpent tongue from the hippie's pale body and wrapped it instead around the firm, strong truck driver.

He waved her closer and whispered, "Stuffed Honduran parrots. Smuggled 'em up through Mexico, highly equitable merchandise."

She purred lithely, her voice quivering, rubbing her body to the floor. She melted into a puddle of crimson flesh, her entire being transformed into one giant erogenous zone.

"Can we get the check when you have a chance?" The trucker was unamused by her antics.

She recomposed herself and slid the check onto the table, scurrying off in an air of contempt.

The truck driver and the long-hair found themselves short of cash and had to stiff the waitress' tip. They nearly made it to the door before she transformed back into a seven-headed fire-breathing serpent and toasted them both.

At that moment, she saw a turtle crawling across the parking lot with an egg balanced on top of its shell. The turtle stopped, and the egg rolled off its back and cracked open on the pavement.

The serpent-waitress looked out, seeing a tiny replica of herself as a human emerging from the broken shell.

The tiny human-waitress looked up at the gigantic serpent, muttered something utterly profound but completely inaudible, and disappeared in a puff of green smoke.

YARN

I was glad when the new family moved into the house a few doors down. I couldn't remember anyone ever living there, and I heard the people moving in had kids. There always seemed to be a lack of kids on my block, so I was excited for new playmates, even after I learned they were quite a bit younger than me.

This turned to my advantage, as it meant I finally got a chance at babysitting. A few weeks after moving in, the Flauberts offered to pay me to watch Keeley and Kyle while they went out for the evening one Saturday night, five dollars an hour. Immediately my brain was working out the math and making timelines of what I could afford and how long I would have to work before I was well-off.

I was so excited by the prospect of making money that I mostly forgot how creepy their house was. When I had gone over to interview for the babysitting job, being inside that house had made my skin crawl, and I couldn't explain why, what it was about the little wooden house that raised the hairs on the back of my neck.

Friday night came, and I was too excited to sleep much. I stayed as still as I could under blankets and tried to let my brain relax. The few times I felt the thoughts chased out of my head by the darkness and quiet, I followed them as best I could toward a dream.

Invariably something would knock me out of this drifting toward sleep, a noise somewhere in the house, a bright light from a passing car, or the old tree just outside my window, leaning in close against the cold and wind, reaching out a bony wooden hand and tapping its fingers against the glass. The old tree wanted my attention, it wanted me awake, but when it whispered its warnings to me in slow, silent sentences, the pace seemed to hypnotize me. Its words were so soft I had to completely quiet my mind, or my own thoughts would drown out the tree's dialogue.

I found myself wide awake, clinging under covers to my pillow. My eyes refused to stay closed any longer. I had been trying so hard to sleep, and my eyes and the rest of my body were now protesting this charade. My body was awake, and my eyes stared out into the black.

There was a hum. A light buzzing or grinding, it was just barely audible above the sound of my own heart. It seemed to be coming from the window, but I couldn't tell if it was the glass rattling or a sound coming from farther outside.

I threw the blankets aside, and the cold ripped at my skin. I crawled out of the bed as spry and quiet as I could be. I snuck to the window the way a cat might approach a mouse.

I felt the vibration on the glass more than I could hear it. It was most definitely coming from outside. I was surprised to see a light on. And I quickly discerned the light was coming from the upstairs of the Flauberts' house a few doors down, its window and mine facing each other directly.

I wasn't sure of the time, but I knew it was terribly late, almost early. The whole world seemed asleep and quiet. Only a few remaining birds who had yet to fly south sat up late singing their songs about staying up late singing on the electric line. A few hints of morning's blue were creeping on the horizon.

I watched the light from the upstairs of the Flauberts' house, wondering who might be awake over there. There was a silhouette in the window that seemed to be active. Whoever it was looked busy, the repeating movements of the shadows dancing. It struck me that this was the source of the humming, the low, dull vibration I could feel more than hear.

I was reminded how uneasy that house made me feel. I was in it for the first time the day before, and it had weighed on me immediately. I couldn't quite place what it was; it came on like the headaches you get from staring too long at the sun or watching too much TV, a small, sharp, pulsing pain that let me know I was not welcome. The house had told me it wanted me to leave.

I sat and watched the shadow, gently rocking, almost like it was in prayer. The dark gray movement against the curtain made it impossible to see what the shadow was doing, or who it was. The quiet electric hum spread out into the night.

I must have fallen asleep with my head against the window. Next thing I knew, my cheek felt burning hot. I opened my eyes and saw the sun looking in, shining through the window right on me.

Mom was calling me for breakfast.

I trod downstairs to the kitchen and slumped into a chair. Dad was over the stove finishing eggs and didn't see me. Mom came in from the back. "Morning, sweetie, did you not sleep well?"

"Uh-uh." I shook my head, and hair flopped over my eyes.

"Are you nervous about your babysitting job tonight?"

"No, there was a noise." I was hesitant to say too much, unsure now how much was a dream and what it would sound like if I tried to explain. "It was quiet, but it kept going all night, like something buzzing."

Dad turned around and carelessly pointed toward me with the greasy spatula. "You see? I told you I heard something. It sounded like a sewing machine, didn't it?"

"I'm not sure," I murmured. "I guess it could have."

"I heard the same thing." He flipped the eggs over one at a time, each one splashing lightly onto the pan, shooting grease and smoke into the air. "It was like a really old sewing machine, like it had a bad ground. It's been years since I'd heard it. Your mother was calling me crazy."

Mom was balancing her coffee cup in the air with two fingers, but her eyes were set on a crossword puzzle. "I don't know. Maybe the Flauberts found Mrs. Grisby's old machine in the attic."

"Who is Mrs. Grisby?" I asked.

Mom put her paper aside, took off her glasses and rubbed at her eyes. "Mrs. Grisby lived in the house the Flauberts moved into. She passed away... I guess it would have been about eight years ago. You're probably too young to remember her."

"Some people say the house is haunted now," Dad teased in the singsong voice he used when he was playfully trying to coax Mom into one of her lectures. "That's why the house sat empty so long."

Mom rolled her eyes and clicked her tongue. "Ghosts."

"You... you don't think it's really haunted, then?" I tried to let my words come out in a detached way, not like I really cared but like I was only curious.

"Of course not, honey." Mom was recommitting herself to her crossword; there would be no lecture this morning. "I don't believe in any of that nonsense, ghosts or aliens or Bigfoot or the boogeyman."

"Me neither." I tried to sound convincing, but I was trying to convince myself. I had no idea what I really believed.

"Mrs. Grisby used to run her sewing machine well into the night." Dad was placing plates of eggs and bacon and toast and fried potatoes in the middle of the table. "She kept to herself, so we never really got to know her, and I guess she didn't have much family to speak of. But she certainly kept active. Almost every night you could look up at that window and see her silhouette against the curtain, rocking back and forth, working the pedals and feeding the fabric. The hum of her ancient and probably badly wired sewing machine would permeate the whole neighborhood."

My stomach felt like it had deflated, shriveled and shrunk into my intestines, acids eating away at my organs, a cramped pain in the gaps between all the bones in my body. My head was spinning, and my skin seemed to tighten and wring cold sweat out of every pore.

"You okay, honey?" Mom had taken off her glasses and was looking closely at me. "You look pale. Are you running a fever?"

She touched my forehead, and the almost frozen sweat came off into her hand, between every finger. She still studied me quizzically, wiping her fingers with a paper towel.

I didn't say anything. I didn't know what to say. I hesitated and decided I wouldn't mention the shadow in the Flauberts' upstairs window. I didn't want her to laugh or think less of me, or especially think me crazy.

"We'll have to see how you feel." Mom leaned in and touched her hand, first the front and then the back, to my cheeks and either side of my neck. "If you're sick, I'm not going to let you babysit for the Flauberts. We'll have to see how you feel in a few hours, okay?"

"Okay," I muttered back. Fear unraveled and fell away from me; every bone, muscle and hair seemed relieved at the notion I could possibly get out of babysitting Keeley and Kyle, of going to the apparently haunted house that hated me.

As the day wore on, my nerves seemed to dissipate, or perhaps the thought of the money I would make superseded the fear. By late afternoon I had mostly forgotten about the scare from the night before, and I wasn't entirely sure that it wasn't just a dream.

It was barely hinting at darkness when I walked over to the Flauberts'. Mrs. Flaubert welcomed me and showed me around the house. Keeley and Kyle scrambled around behind her, clearly wanting to observe me but too timid to do it in the open. We went from the kitchen through the hallway and past the stairs to the large open front room.

"Our bedroom is at the end of the hall," Mrs. Flaubert told me, waving an arm toward the closed door, "and the kids share this room. We don't use the upstairs at all yet." She tried to sound casual, but there was something forced in her voice. I couldn't tell what it was, but the room seemed suddenly cold. I felt nervous for the first time since I'd arrived. Keeley and Kyle seemed to lose a bit of their curiosity as well; they hung well out of the way, peeking out from behind the living room couch. Neither smiled.

"We shouldn't be much later than midnight," Mrs. Flaubert continued, trying to cut through the icy feeling blanketing the room. "They've already had dinner, but a few cookies or a snack later on is fine. They should be good and tired, and they usually go to bed around ten thirty, but they can stay up and wait for us if they want. They can watch something on TV or put in a movie."

The bedroom door opened and shut quickly. Mr. Flaubert was mostly a blur of motion, barely acknowledging any of us. A quick round of polite greetings and gestures, and the adults were gone.

I stood alone in the kitchen watching the back door close behind them, and I could feel Keeley and Kyle approaching me now. I turned and saw them peeking into the room, shielded by the refrigerator. Their two heads, one over the other; they were twins, but Keeley was so much taller than Kyle. She seemed almost tall enough to be the same age as me, but her reserved and shy demeanor indicated her true age and maturity.

I smiled large at the both of them, trying to appear at ease and easygoing. They warmed slightly. Kyle maintained eye contact when I looked directly at him, where he had previously averted his gaze and kept his attention shifting. He stepped out in front of the refrigerator and returned the smile but still kept his head slightly down and looked self-conscious.

"So, what do you guys want to do?" I asked.

"We can watch cartoons!" Kyle shouted.

Keeley stepped out from behind the fridge and put her hand on her brother's shoulder. "We should think of a game to play," she said.

"Let's play Lava!" Kyle blurted, just as enthusiastic as he had been about cartoons.

I had never heard of the game. "What's that?"

"It's where we pretend the ground is covered in hot lava," Keeley explained. "So you have to stay on the couch or on a chair, or anywhere you go you can't touch the ground or you'll get burned up."

"Oh yeah," I said, "we always just called that Don't Touch the Ground."

Kyle had already scurried sideways through the hallway and was scrambling to get up on the couch.

"I don't want to play Lava." Keeley stood firm where she was and now crossed her arms. "I can just sit on the chair and watch TV and say I won. Let's play a game where we actually have to do something."

Kyle had stomped back into the hall and was looking at Keeley and me, waiting for official instruction.

"We could play hide and seek," I offered.

"Yeah!" Kyle was excited for anything, he didn't care what. He just wanted to play.

"That sounds okay," said Keeley. "Can we hide inside and outside?"

I shrugged. "It's your guys' house, so you can set the boundaries."

"I think we can hide inside or outside," she replied, "but not outside our yard." And then quietly she added, "Or upstairs."

Kyle nodded in strong agreement.

"Does someone live upstairs?" I asked, wanting some confirmation of what I thought I saw or dreamed the previous night. "Your grandma or someone?"

"No one lives upstairs." Keeley's words crawled out of her mouth without emotion. "We don't go upstairs at all. Kyle thinks it's haunted."

Kyle nodded more strongly now, blond hair flipping back and bouncing from his forehead.

"Haunted?" I tried to remain calm and brave.

"I don't believe in ghosts." Keeley rolled her eyes slightly at her brother.

"Me neither. I don't believe in ghosts either," I said to convince myself as much as the kids.

"Okay," Keeley was bold again, instructing her brother, "okay. Bathroom is Glue. Kyle, you count to a hundred in there, and we'll hide."

The boy traipsed to the other end of the hall and closed the door behind him. Immediately we heard him begin to count, slow and pronounced.

Keeley and I met eyes for a moment. She gave me a sparkling half-smile and ducked out and away, crossing the kitchen.

I glanced around. Here, the kitchen, stairs and bathroom door; at the other end, the kitchen led out to the living room and met both bedroom doors. Kyle still counted loudly through the door behind me. "Eleven... twelve... thirteen..."

I heard the back door shut. Keeley had tried to pull it shut as slowly and silently as possible, but the wood door sliding against its frame betrayed her.

I darted through the hall and looked in at the living room. A couch to hide behind, and the TV was big enough that if I ducked under the bay window curtain I might go unnoticed. The whole house was unfamiliar, and part of me wanted to look at as little of it as possible.

"Nineteen... twenty... twenty-one..."

My heart beat extra-hard and felt like it might burst through my shirt. I turned and faced upward, toward the door at the top of the stairs. An almost irresistible curiosity swept over me. The golden brown carpeting of the hall and living room continued up the stairs but grew darker and shadowed. An almost ugly, plain wooden door hid unlit at the top.

"Twenty-seven... Twenty-eight... Twenty-nine..."

My stomach swam in a circle inside my skin. I found it terrifying; it wasn't so much anything about the house that frightened me, but rather my sudden inability to resist the curiosity. It wasn't a feeling or a notion or an urge or anything emotional. It was an undeniable necessity. I couldn't stop my legs when I saw them shuffling under me and climbing the steps. A cold sweat snuck out between my hair and my forehead, and my heart seemed to be knocking directly on my eardrums every time it fluttered. I had to know what was upstairs, why it was closed off, why everyone including me felt afraid of it. I had to know.

I stopped for a breath in the shadow at the top of the stairs. I laid a palm on the door. Nothing felt strange. I wasn't sure what I had expected.

"Forty... forty-one... forty-two..." Kyle's voice sounded quieter from up here. I also think he may have started to lose his excitement.

I reached up and gripped the cold metal doorknob. I closed my eyes as hard as they would go, somehow thinking it would make me quieter. I twisted the knob, deliberately and delicately, praying and hoping the door wouldn't make any noise as I pushed it open.

Kyle's muted counting drifted out of range as I slipped up into the darkness.

The door swung away by itself and clicked quietly back into place. I opened my eyes. A scream flew out of my throat when I saw the clown staring at me. I saw the frame and realized it was only a painting. I hoped I hadn't given myself away. I think I barely screamed at all. I tried to open my eyes as wide as they would go, as if this would somehow let them adjust to the darkness more quickly.

The painting still stared down at me. I was light-headed or something. The giant round red nose pulsated, and the clown appeared to swim flat against the wall, one eye at a time bulging. My heart was trying to break free through my throat.

I reached back and felt the doorknob in my grip. I yanked it, but it refused to budge, the metal clicking a disgruntled negative. I had locked myself upstairs.

I felt sick and dizzy. The clown silently laughed at me. Bristling bright colors seemed to dance as if windswept in tiny breezes on the velvet surface, tracing the round border of his lips, which contained his teeth and the rest of the darkness behind them. The lips themselves seemed too bright, nearly glowing against the shadows, as if covered in blood that dripped slowly toward the clown's chin.

I had to turn away. I stumbled into the main part of the room to get away from the painting. I was pooled in a gray glow, the bright white moon, nearly full, and the streetlamps outside shining in through the window and the plain white curtain. I felt better for some reason when I saw the window. Probably mostly for the silhouette of the outside world and the dull glow of light it afforded me.

I crept slowly toward the window and saw the small wooden table leaning against the wall directly under the length of the curtain. Something about the table told me it was older than almost anything I had yet encountered in my short life. Something that seemed to be dust or smoke danced chaotically in the moonlight wave that rolled in toward me.

I heard the crickets calling from outside. I heard the highway past the end of the block. I tried to concentrate on any sounds that might be coming from inside the house. I was pretty sure Kyle was done counting and was now trying to find his sister or me.

I had heard her slip outside and figured it might take him some time to find her. But I thought about Kyle being afraid of the upstairs and felt slightly reassured that I still had a little time to find a niche to creep into so I could stay well out of light and out of sight.

I swiveled from the window and saw a door with slatted wooden vents like a rib cage. I crossed the room toward it and pulled the handle quietly but hard, and I saw the outline of a few winter coats, a floor riddled with boots and single gloves. I was relieved it was a closet; I'm not sure why.

I carefully swung my leg past the threshold and then pulled the rest of my body into the closet.

I was wrapped completely in black. Again I tried to open my eyes as wide as they would go, vainly attempting to see something in the dark. Little pulses of white flashed on my eyeballs, my brain compensating for so little light. I seemed to be sinking.

The white sparks in my field of vision flashed and pulsed faster, and my legs didn't want to hold me upright anymore. A wave of red, nearly black and barely discernible from the dark, scrolled down in front of me, and then another one. I darted my eyes, but they couldn't focus, couldn't see anything outside of my head, the waves of dirty blood or dark electric static. The dark surrounded me, confronting me.

My limbs didn't feel attached to anything. I was falling; the ground around me had disintegrated in the darkness. I flailed my legs, and they kicked around, hitting against walls and clothes. My stomach untied itself from my intestines, and a salty venom poured on every nerve end. I couldn't even scream. The pulse continued flashing against black.

I reached an arm out, hopeful to grab on to anything. Behind me my fingers knocked at the slatted wooden door, in front of me my other hand grabbed something that felt like fur. I tried to make a fist, to grab a hold of whatever it was, but my fingers refused to cooperate.

My throat felt like it was squeezing shut against a lump of chalk. I could barely breathe, managing only a few shallow gasps. The cold air attacked my throat and lungs like frozen shards of glass. Still I seemed to be falling, but the door behind me remained still. I was pretty sure the drop was only imagined. Even seeing the tiny light pouring in through the slats didn't ease the feeling that I was still falling fast. Red, frozen wind raced past my ears.

My hand in front reached into fur and fabric, grasping for something solid enough to hang onto. Inside a coat, under the cloth, my fingers felt something hard, a wooden hanger. I gripped and it slipped out of my hand. I lost my balance. Both arms flailed now, knocking against the dark, and metal squeaked against metal. Everything seemed to be sliding away from me. My knees hit the ground, and something heavy and thick fell on top of me. I couldn't see anything, and I seemed tied in a knot on the closet floor. Any way I tried to move, any limbs I tried to work were firmly stuck in place, unable to budge. Not even a scream could escape from this pile; a thick fold of fabric had wrapped around my head and covered my mouth, keeping me silent against the oppressive darkness blanketing me.

Faintly and far off I heard a scream. I wondered for a moment if it was mine, if I had managed to make some sound after all. I tried to scream again but couldn't. With bristles of fur in my mouth, I couldn't help but inhale wet, hot, sloppy air. Each of my limbs was either pinned under me or wrapped tightly in fabric. I couldn't fight my way out. I tried to scream again, but still only impotent wind limped from my mouth. I couldn't see anything but the wash of reddish black waves sweeping over me. They seemed in pace with my heart. A hard, pounding beat in my chest, pierced by every breath, coordinated with the waves flashing in my vision.

I wasn't sure if my eyes were open or shut. I was pretty sure I was on the closet floor, but most of my body still felt like I was falling headlong and crashing toward nothing.

I saw a flash of light, followed by a peal of thunder. I still couldn't escape, but I stopped struggling so I could listen. Between the heartbeats something seemed to be creaking. A steady patter of water against metal told me it was raining.

I felt there was something upstairs with me, and the faint creaking, squeaking sound I heard suggested I was not alone. I remained as calm and still as possible, keeping my ears alert as I tried to gather what was happening and who was with me now.

The room seemed calm, almost silent. I struggled to get my arms or legs free, still not really sure what they were entangled in. I grasped some cloth, and possibly a coat hanger within, and squeezed to hang on tight, when something cracked. It felt like bone and shattered between my fingers. It crumbled to dust and fell around me. A warm terror crawled up my spine.

I heard the creaking again between breaths, the patter of light rain outside. Another sound emerged: a low hum, a quiet grinding. An electric, motorized buzzing. I remained absolutely still, not wishing to give away my hiding place. My eyes stung, burnt by some chemical, I blinked and still saw only dark, only remnants of light from within my own mind. I could hear my own heartbeat, and I could watch it too, manifested as the bloody black wave scrolling past my field of vision.

I wasn't sure how long I'd been hiding. I wondered if I could count the heartbeats backwards to determine how much time had passed since I'd made my way upstairs. Over my head there was a flash of light, followed shortly by another rolling crack of thunder. The sound faded back toward silence until only my heartbeat and the raindrops continued.

More clatter, more commotion crashed through the darkness. I tried to untangle from the coiled knot of scarves and winter jackets and black. I released an arm from its trap and boosted myself into a sitting position, where I could peer out through the lowest slats of the wooden closet door.

A dim light meandered in, past the yellowing curtain, flapping and dancing in the wind, letting the moonlight come in out of the rain.

The hum became louder, prominently electric, covering me, but still I saw nothing else but the window on the wall opposite me and the wooden table resting right under it. Strange random shapes and monsters played out on the wall, and the curtain buckled and flapped, making ominous silhouettes dance in shadow.

A figure approached the window and the table. I saw it was Keeley, but she didn't see me. She was focused on the window, and I was silently cowering in the closet. The back of her dress billowed, and her long blond locks seemed to coil more like a living creature than a head of hair.

Keeley turned sharply and stared. I could feel her eyes on me.

"This is my house!" she hissed, but it wasn't her voice. It wasn't the voice of a preteen girl; it was a wooden, decrepit voice, smokey and cold. Something was wrong with her appearance as well. I had to squint, and it was still so dark, but she looked to have two heads. Not one on top of the other like a totem pole, but two heads in the same physical space. The young girl with the pale face and slightly rosy cheeks, blond curls of yarn hanging from her temples; and a faded face, a bright white, reflected head that appeared only half real, a blurred monstrosity that spoke with a voice scraped off a ship's anchor, barnacles and broken glass bottles.

"This will always be my house!" the old voice called out. It made me dizzy to see both heads occupying the same area, one fading to let the other shine. Keeley seemed to disappear when the voice was speaking, and a prominent profile showed chalky granite features, an ancient existence come back to take over a young body.

Keeley, or Keeley's body, was approaching me slowly. I saw she held a long, metal instrument in one hand, shiny and bright, a pair of knitting needles glinting in the moonlight. The two heads came together at her eyes, strong and solid and open much too wide, staring precisely at me. From there the two heads lost substance and faded from view and reality, fighting each other for control.

I tried to back away from the door and burrow deeper into the closet. I hit the back wall, but the closet door swung open. Keeley stood directly in front of me, one hand wielding a knitting needle, her eyes possessed, blond locks blowing chaotically, dancing above her head, twisting and flailing and tying themselves into and out of knots. The electric hum in the background became prominent. The eyes in the middle of Keeley's face flared red. "You will all leave my house and leave me alone!"

She continued to creep toward me. I heard feet on the stairs and heard Kyle shouting, "You leave my sister alone! Get away from my sister!"

Kyle made his way into the room, throwing any object at hand at Keeley. Most were naturally missing her, and the rest she batted away with her free hand. The eyes burning in the middle of her head never wavered from their direct, intensive attention on me. She continued to slowly approach.

Kyle kept yelling and throwing books at her. He had the clown painting in his hands now and was preparing to fling it at her like a Frisbee.

He let the painting fly, and the spirit controlling Keeley's body finally looked away, putting an arm up against the painting. I tried to pull myself up and retreat farther back into the closet.

A loud crack told me I had hit my head on the wall. A sharp jolt of pain shocked my whole body, Kyle's shout faded away, my vision of him fell out of focus, and darkness swam and came together in my periphery. Keeley was fading from vision as well, both the heads fighting for space, flashing one to the other, the young girl and the old monster, the scared preteen and the old soul that had once inhabited this home. Everything disappeared. All sight and sound swept up into the electric hum, which was all that seemed to be real anymore.

It was just after midnight when the adult Flauberts returned. I thought they would be mad at how they found us. I was still pressed up against the back of the upstairs closet, and Kyle was sleeping out in the toolshed in the backyard and woke up when he heard the car pull up. Keeley was asleep in a rocking chair in front of the upstairs window. I hadn't seen the rocking chair, and Mrs. Flaubert seemed frightened at the sight of it. She wasn't sure how Keeley had managed to get it down from the attic, as it weighed almost a hundred pounds.

Mrs. Flaubert paid me and walked me home, mostly in silence. I felt guilty, but I wasn't even sure what had happened or why. I guess I kept expecting her to be mad at me for going upstairs. But she didn't lecture me or scold me or even give me a disappointed look. She seemed mostly scared and nervous, still shocked by the sight she had come home to.

She asked again if I was okay, and I limply nodded. Her eyes danced around for anything I might not be telling. She watched me go inside the house and then returned to her own.

I couldn't sleep much at all through the night, still terrified but uncertain what I had really experienced. I never saw any of the Flauberts again.

My mom told me when I woke up late the next afternoon that the Flauberts had left. She asked me what happened, and I only meekly shook my head. She said they had decided to leave, to let the house go and move somewhere else, but they didn't say why.

I sat alone in my bed most of the day and into the evening. I tried not to think about the night before. I couldn't tell what I had seen or if it was real. I wondered what the Flauberts had actually seen when they came home, and what Keeley or

Kyle may have told the adults. Icy nerves swam in my stomach when I thought of the darkness and the crazy dreamlike spectacle, of Keeley and old Mrs. Grisby occupying the same space, stalking and tormenting me.

I wondered where the Flauberts might go, where they might wind up. And if I would ever find out what really happened. What was I supposed to tell people about that night?

I finally got out of bed late in the evening. I went downstairs and wandered into the kitchen, expecting my mom or dad to be there, but it was empty. I looked around the house and realized I was the only one home. I didn't want to be alone.

Outside the front door I saw a few faces and glints of light. A small gathering was collecting outside the Flauberts' empty house.

I saw my parents lingering on the perimeter and jumped outside, crossing the yard and the driveway. I felt safe and secure once I was in my dad's presence. He ran his hand through my hair and gave me a comforting pat. "One day you're going to have to tell us what happened," he said. It wasn't a threat or a demand; there was a sort of curious air in his voice, an awe I hadn't often heard. "The Flauberts seemed scared out of their minds when they drove off this morning."

We stood there, looking up at the house, at the yellowing paper curtain in the second-floor window, flapping and curling against the breeze. And behind the curtain, the dark gray silhouette, the figure rocking slowly, the shadow of the old woman who still commanded an authority. And the hum of the old sewing machine pulsing, echoing against the dark of night.

AMERICAN IDLE

I recently won first prize on the newest reality television competition, *American Idle*. I say it here not to brag, but because I realize most of you probably missed it.

Admittedly, it was an extremely boring program and was only aired in the unrespected hours of the morning on cable channels, when the *Girls Gone Wild* people and the peddlers of diet drugs and male-enhancement pills had all run out of money to hawk their titillating wares.

The series was a competition to find the laziest person in America, no easy feat by any means. Most of the contestants disqualified themselves simply by showing up; something I had thought about doing but never quite got around to.

In the end, I believe it was the essay I wrote on slothfulness that put me over the top in the eyes of the judges. They had asked for a five-thousand-word dissertation on the merits of utter inertia; I turned in one half-assed paragraph, and three weeks past deadline to boot. One cannot fake that sort of apathy.

Here is what I composed:

"Weary of it all; so much to say, but...
who has the time? Just pulling my body
from the bed this afternoon has
expended all my energy;
perhaps after a nap..."

And with that, I thrust my way into the annals of reality television superstardom. Look for me soon on the talk show circuit (not the really early ones, mind you).

And start your Christmas shopping early, as I can tell you this season's must-have toy, the one people will line up for on Black Friday at five in the morning and trample over each other to get to. The toy they'll be giggling about on the news, when they tell you tales of holiday shoppers stabbing each other in the aisle, fighting over the last of the *Robert Emmett American Idle Inaction Figures*.

GOD'S WRITING GROUP

God's writing group met on Sundays. He planned His whole week around it.

One day He was at the *Tetra-Mocha-Ton* early (just 'coffee,' no frills), muttering, scribbling a few words with His quill and then invariably scratching them out.

Randy and Mandy came in and were standing in line to place their order before settling in to write. Randy noticed God first; he gave a little tug at Mandy's elbow and gestured for her to look. They both stood silently, watching God fret and fume over the page in front of Him. They both smiled a little to see Him so agitated.

"Does He ever have any fun?" Mandy whispered. "I mean, He does know a hobby is supposed to be an enjoyable activity, doesn't He?"

Randy shook his head and shrugged. "I admire His dedication and sometimes envy His intensity, but I don't even take my job as seriously as He takes writing."

Mandy chuckled. They got their drinks and joined God at the table.

"How's the story coming, God?" Randy asked, smiling a little too widely to be mistaken for sincere. "Looks like You're still having a little trouble there."

God grumbled and offered half a wave of His hand, consumed by the words before Him.

"It's a rough spot, but You'll get through it," Mandy tried to placate Him. "It will make a good book. I think You have a winner. You were very excited about it, and that first week of writing was incredible, almost miraculous."

"Yeah..." God let the word out as a long sigh. He put His quill into the barrel and rubbed a fist at

His tired eyes. He finally looked up at His friends and attempted a smile.

"Some of those characters You've introduced..." Randy didn't finish his thought. He let the fragmented idea linger, let the silence convey what he hesitated to say.

"They've taken on lives of their own," God said. "I can't get them to behave and stay within the story I have planned."

Mandy hit God on the shoulder, softly. "You see? God knows what I mean! Sometimes the characters do surprise us! No matter how much you outline, when you get into the writing, you can be surprised by who your characters really turn out to be and the places they'll go when they should be moving the plot forward!"

Randy clicked his tongue and rolled his eyes. "This again. You are the writer. You made the characters. Anything they do is a product of your imagination, and to believe otherwise, to talk about them like they are sentient beings, is delusional and possibly hints at a serious mental imbalance."

"So you're never surprised by any of your characters or any of your stories?" Mandy kept her gaze on Randy, awaiting his reply while removing her laptop from its case and opening it on the table.

"Of course I've been surprised," Randy replied, still smiling widely. "But I recognize that the surprises are a product of my own mind. I don't pretend that my characters are acting on their own."

"You are so literal." Mandy moved Styrofoam cups and a glass of water away from her computer. The screen lit up, and a phrase of warm piano let her know the laptop was now awake. "And you say God takes things too seriously."

God was still immersed in His work, writing three words and then crossing out four. But at the mention of His name, He looked up and glanced between Randy and Mandy.

"I know it comes from me," Mandy continued. "It's just a bit of fun, really. The ideas come from our subconscious. We are not actively making these choices, so it seems like the characters are doing it. Plus, it sounds vain if I say, 'Look what I thought up!' It's so much nicer to say, 'Look what my characters did!'" Mandy laughed as she finished her last thought, involuntarily kicking at a table leg and knocking over the glass of water.

She threw the few available napkins on the growing puddle and got up quickly to find something better to clean up the mess.

God looked at Randy for a few tense moments before He spoke. "I really don't control what my characters do anymore. I let them go. I think you've read the garden scene where I gave them all free will."

Randy regarded his friend, curious and somber, his wry smile replaced by a relief map of worry lines on his forehead and a slight squinting of his eyes. "You do know that's not true, don't You? There is no 'free will.' You do know that is only a plot device, right? You are doing all of this. It's from Your mind. You are the writer of this story."

God said nothing but stared back at Randy. There was something new in His eyes, but Randy couldn't place it. It unnerved him, but he couldn't say why.

God glanced at the overturned glass still lying on the table and the slow pool of water soaking into the napkins.

"Maybe you're right, Randy," He finally replied, quiet and calm and steady. He took up His quill once more and hunched over the page, returning to His work. "Maybe you're right. Here comes the flood."

JETTISON

Stopping into a restaurant, we find that we have stumbled upon one of those new and infamous Psychoanalytical Delicatessens where instead of simply ordering your food, you are instead given an examination and interview touching a broad spectrum of subjects. Your meal is then prepared based on your mental-health diagnosis arrived at by your waitress.

Simple cases get the blunt fruits, bananas or nuts, watermelon cheese soup. I usually have a dish called 'Manic Tension over easy, side of Grandeur, extra Inner Uterine Memories'. It's a casserole/skillet creation, consisting mostly of large black things that taste like burnt rubber. After years of enjoying the recipe, the only ingredient I could identify was fried cricket torso.

Remember when we all started evolving our sixth fingers? An extra thumb, on the other side. We called it the 'supposing thumb,' since we mostly sat staring at it, wondering what it was for.

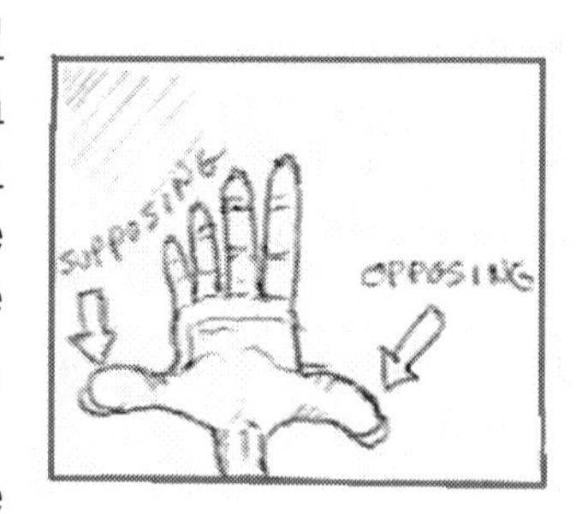

We find ourselves in the dining room, with only the heavy wooden table and the chairs containing us around it.

We sit for hours in relative quiet, and we clean up after ourselves, or at least keep our messes self-contained around us in little piles.

Now that we have this moment alone together, there are probably some things I should explain.

The doors are shut and silent, and the constant ruckus of people coming and going has finally stopped.

The radio in the background is just noticeable, spilling out unobtrusive melodies; the music doesn't dare to slip between us, to interrupt the gaze we share. An ash tray overflowing, three days of butts, smoldering, a sticky nicotine haze that separates me from you. Much more, but I don't know how to say it.

The building burning down around us almost makes it feel like summer. Your eyes floating, beautiful in the dish on the table, dyed blue. I think we are still waiting for dessert, and I know we are waiting for spring to come and carry us away.

Maybe I'm just drunk, too tired to swim for the words I need, under the table spillings. Tomorrow they'll sweep all this away, and only then will they know what I was trying to say, what I was really thinking, how I felt. If only I could tell you now, lift this linoleum sheath and show you what sits under it.

I mean, there are some things that shouldn't be left up to assumption.

The fact that we met only earlier this week, though we both know we've met before. Not recently, not even in this lifetime. But we both know we've wandered with each other backwards through time.

I think we were once rats, a long time ago, living off the same garbage heap, feeding on the same plague victims. Those were the days, do you remember?

You exit through the walkway that leads above the parking lot past the bad motel with two rates for rooms, one for orgies and one for overdosing.

They're shouting at us now, my sand-baggy love, calling from the street below, telling us to evacuate. Telling us to call someone collect. Telling us to at least listen. Their words are absorbed by the coral sponges we spread over the windows, and we're losing oxygen too quickly to worry about it anymore.

You've returned with a quantum eraser, a strange muddy mess of particles, a subatomic demagnetizer. You rub it against my mouth.

"That should shut you up for a while," you wink a ruthless grin.

I find a crayon and draw a mouth as fast as possible before I suffocate.

"эюЯəоЂƷбЪ!" comes out of the new orifice. I've drawn it sideways or skewed somehow.

You rub your eraser to my face. But I keep drawing new mouths as frantically as I can.

I've got a half dozen holes in my head, all babbling chaos at you, before you regroup and erase my hands.

THE NEW GUISE

The last orange lock hit the shower floor. I ran my hand across my scalp, hot water penetrating the skin under my hair for the first time in years. I felt lighter. My skull was no longer choking, strangled in a noose of knots, the budding dreadlocks that fell from my head.

I turned off the water and stepped out. I wrapped a towel around my head and pulled it tight, shaking the last of the water from my body. They were going to be shocked, if they even recognized me.

I rubbed the towel against the mirror, cut a small circle into the steam so I could see my face. I stuck my tongue toward the glass; it was pink, and my teeth were white. Fresh bare skin where my beard and mustache had been, soft and smooth.

A new coat of fog was building on the mirror. I toweled my limbs and made for the clothes. On the floor the old pile crumbled like a dead clown, the green plaid golf pants and the tie-dyed t-shirt of the triangle on the back of a dollar bill. Bright blending shapes and waves of fading color. One pink shoe and one purple shoe sat on top.

The new jeans felt too heavy, and their blue seemed too bright. It had been a while since I had worn anything this new. I topped a white undershirt with an even whiter dress shirt. I buttoned it from the bottom up, and also the cuffs.

I caught a glimpse of myself in the mirror. I was beginning to look normal. Glints of metal rang in the light. I reached up and pulled the studs and hoops from each ear.

I wiped the mirror clear again, sat down on the toilet and pulled the black shoes onto my feet, tying them properly and snug.

I clipped the rest of my hair down to a half-inch; once it was dry I applied the temporary dye. The top of my head turned to black, used like a match. I touched at my eyebrows to give them some color.

I was almost completely transformed.

I pulled on a shiny black leather jacket and touched at my hair once more. I barely recognized the reflection staring back at me. I laughed for a minute, saw the corner of the mouth curl up. The proper stranger laughing from across the glass was laughing at me as well.

I shut all the lights off in the bathroom and made my way back into the kitchen. Outside, evening was coming; the bright daylight faded to a deep blue. It was time to set the plans in motion. It was time to find the party.

In the bedroom I gave myself one final glance in the full-length mirror, and then I slipped my keys and cash into the front pocket of my jeans.

I was out in the night, strolling up the street. The chill of summer's end was still floating in the night air, and it didn't feel quite so cold, but slightly drier, slightly sharper. I couldn't see my breath, at least. I exhaled nothing back into the night. I passed under a streetlamp and felt momentarily visible again.

On the other side of town, at the end of the one-way cul-de-sac, the one with no legal way in, there was a party, in the house at the funny angle on the hill.

I crept up the sidewalk and saw shapes and shadows on the window, a warm, inviting chaos from within the house. I could hear the music rattling glass and shingles. Conversations cresting and flowing, roars of laughter exploding at random. I was ready for a party.

I knocked at the door and put the best smile I could muster as high on my face as it would fit. It took a minute or so until someone opened the door.

"Uh, hey," a pot-bellied guy with a beard and a weeping willow wig blinked out at me. He dragged a long drink from an oversized beer can. I didn't recognize him.

"Hey, man. Happy Halloween!" I held out my hand, out and then up, in case he would shake my hand or high-five me or something, but he only watched my hand flop in silent curiosity. "Here to party, man! Looks like you guys have it well underway."

The guy at the door stared at me and chewed slowly on something. "Who are you? Who do you know here?"

"It's me, man, Slogan." I tried to emphasize earnest truth. "Everybody knows me. Dangle and Dafne, Fezby, Puner, Dentist, Purple, Sedna, Juky, The Guy with the Arm, everyone knows me."

It was getting colder out now. I slammed my fingers into my pockets, but they jammed against a layer of ice at the first knuckle, chafing every finger and threatening to bleed.

"Yeah." He blinked at me again. I wasn't sure if he spoke English or maybe he was on a tape feed and couldn't process the proper file in time. "They're all here, but I still don't know who you are. Hang on, I'm gonna get someone."

"Okay," I said and tried to step into the house, but the pot-bellied man stuck his hand in my way and shook his head.

"You have to wait outside until I know you're okay."

I sighed and accepted it, as wrong as it felt. I didn't know this guy who was guarding the door, but I was glad he was going to get someone else. Most everyone inside would know my name. Most of them know who I am.

I stood on the concrete step, not facing the closed door but looking behind me toward the moon. A small pink moon, just emerging, just waking and small and still sleepy.

The door clicked and opened again.

Fezby stood before me, or someone dressed as Fezby. As dark as it was becoming, it was hard to say for sure. My only light was the yellow plastic porch light and a few dim flashes from the fireflies. I reached my hand out to offer to him in peace.

"What's up, man?" He nodded once, acknowledged my hand but wouldn't take it. "What's going on?"

"It's me, dude. It's Slogan." I chuckled and urged him with my honesty. "I don't know that guy who answered the door, but he wouldn't let me in."

"Yeah, I don't know who you think you are, but you've got the wrong party, dude." He turned and let the door go, disregarding me completely.

"Fezby! It's me, Slogan!"

He turned back, held the door ajar with two fingers. Behind him a few people were congregating at the door, expecting a show. He measured me completely from head to toe silently and shook his head. "Slogan's not here, man, although he should be. I'm not sure who you are, but I'll tell him you stopped by."

"Dude, Fezby, It's me, man! I am Slogan!"

He looked at me again, deliberate and careful, sideways and somewhat distracted. I realized what he was doing: he wasn't even really looking at me, he was looking *for* me. He looked just over the top of my head, not at the temporary dyed-black hair, but searching for the sloppy pile of orange dreadlocks he was used to. Less than studying my apparel, he was glancing and averting his gaze from the expected rainbow of colors that usually marked my attire. "Definitely the wrong party, buddy." He called back into the house, "Does anyone know this guy at the door?"

Fezby got a few drunken shouts and random laughter in response and gave me a shrug. He seemed sorry, but the door was closing. He couldn't see me anymore. He wouldn't recognize me.

It didn't matter if I knocked again and got anyone else to answer. None would recognize me this way. Clean and straight and solid and upright.

And even if they somehow trusted that I was supposed to be there, they would still be inspecting me all night and make it impossible to relax. I had gone beyond a costume. I had reorganized my entire being. The person I was dressed as wasn't invited to the party. And unfortunately for me, I had become the person I was dressed as.

I let the music and laughter fade into the background. I gave up and walked back home. I had gone too far. I had become unreal, unhinged.

Even walking home I felt different. I was treated differently. Strangers passing on the street remained on the same side as they walked by. No laughs, no long, curious looks. Costumed clusters of humanity passed me by, blushing. They felt silly in their masks because they didn't realize mine was also a disguise. In passing I even heard a few mumbled whispers, "Good evening, sir. Happy Halloween."

Under each streetlamp on the pathway home, I would reconsider any physical aspects that came into light for a few minutes. Around the corner I climbed upon the bridges of laid wooden two-by-fours and tree trunks. I watched unfamiliar matching shoes, balancing above the rapid water, my laces slipping short from one foot, my heel yanking at an aglet. The lace would certainly unravel before I got back home.

EMMANUEL & ZINA

It was such a long time ago. We were only children playing a game of hide and seek. We would take turns, one of us immersing into illusion and disguise while the other waited, counting, and then came to discover.

We built a little garden, a playground for our game. I went inside and hid amongst the landscapes and the livestock, amongst the elusive passage of time, and many bright and shiny things.

I hid so well I forgot about the game. I mistook my mask for flesh and began to imagine this all was real.

It is only now that I remember why I have been hiding for so long. And I wonder if you are close yet to finding me.

Or are you even looking anymore?

DESTINY

I was never trying to make any statement. I only forgot to take a shower. I've been waiting for so many slow trains and snowstorms that I have no time for hygiene beyond the bottle of mock-perfume air freshener in the glove box.

Watching as the cars go past slowly enough to read the weight limitations and capacity specifications stamped on their steel skin.

I'm cranky from all the chewing gum. I just swabbed down my whole body an hour ago. It took seventeen Wet-Naps to get me all clean. But the stench is already creeping.

Through the plastic lemon scent and the ammonia that tries to push my itchy eyes out of my head, I can already smell death, the crusty fumes of a man rotting from the inside out.

I know if this train were to ever end, there's a truck stop up the way where you can shower in privacy. It's a buck and a quarter for ten minutes. But as far as I can see, an endless procession of train cars, tiny dots on the horizon that gradually grow along the line.

They stretch before me, groaning, smoking and old. I wait and rot. They're adding new cars on at the front end. The shiny, silver boxes will be rusted and squeaking by the time they pass in front of me. Rotten, dilapidated bits of metal that crumble apart, they'll need to be amputated from the back of the train on the other end before slipping over the horizon to die.

I've spent the better part of my life this way, sitting, waiting, helpless. I've felt heavenly inspirations dissipate and dwindle for the goddamned trains. The moment you know you must move. You hear opportunity knocking in your heart, or has it come and gone again?

Mostly I am resigned to the fact that nothing is possible with the grating hypnotic screech of metal on metal. The gate light and bell, alternating left to right, blinking a regular rhythm at me.

I know the only movement I can make is to climb up into a train car. Like they say, if you can't beat them, lie down and let them sweep you away. I've vowed to never step foot on one, not as long as a dim awareness still glows inside my hollowed-out, vacuum-chamber head. I know where the trains end up, and I would rather sit and pensively rot, waiting for the moment that will never come.

I'm trapped, I know. The only escape is to leave my known life behind, abandoning every memory I have and places I've been and with whom; giving up every hope and dream I've managed to hang on to; up the corrugated metal steps, to take me wherever the train will go.

There's nothing else, no other option except to sit and wait and eventually rot away to dust. But I have seen which way those crippled metal boxes go, where they wind up, and I won't dare to make a move.

SEDNA

I sat in the bookstore coffee shop, meditatively sipping at my coffee, flipping through endless blank paper. Merely letting time pass, keeping track of its progression in the methodical turning of pages.

I noticed that the waitress who had originally served me was now seated across from me at the table closest to the door, staring out into the evening and fumbling around with the contents of her purse. She was finished with her shift, watching the parking lot for her ride.

Her eyes darted self-consciously. She bit at her lip and continued to fidget inside her purse. She was still wearing the coffee shop's uniform – an ugly synthetic dress shirt, with drab synthetic colors in bold stripes down the front, and a name tag that read: Sedna.

"That is a very unique name," I said, gaining her attention. "Can I ask where it comes from? What it means?"

She looked at me, glancing sideways. "My real name is Edna," she said with a giggle. "But it's such an old lady's name, so I added the 'S.' Sedna is an Inuit name for the Goddess of the Sea, and it was almost the name of the tenth planet in our solar system, before it dragged Pluto back to planetoid."

I gave an impressed nod but couldn't find a comment.

"What is that you're reading?" she asked.

"An Illustrated Guide to the Indigenous Snake Population of Hawaii."

She furrowed her brow and stared at me, squinting and scrunching her lips as she seemed to work out her reply. "I do a bit of painting myself," she said, "but I like to keep my subjects a little more realistic."

I smiled, impressed by how she called my bluff.

We sat and talked for some time, at first discussing painting and the arts, and then touching on a broad spectrum of subjects. After a while it was apparent that the ride she was waiting for wasn't going to show.

The cafe was closing soon. Lights were turned off here and there, magazines and books were first stacked in separate piles and then carried off and put away. She told me she lived pretty close by but didn't like to walk alone at night. I offered to walk her home.

The small town was utterly silent, all the shops shut up and the traffic gone from the streets. A strangely small and yellow moon poked through an otherwise impenetrably black sky.

She lived on the University's campus. Soon I saw buildings growing out of the dark horizon and scattering around us. We walked on, and she led me toward an odd-looking building. Long, rectangular, and four or five stories tall; and then something that seemed to be perched on top of the building. A large, dark shape that I couldn't quite distinguish from the black of the sky.

"What is that?" I asked Sedna.

"That's the lab where I do my research."

We continued on toward the strange building. A slight breeze drifted around us, settling between us and mingling. An electrical tingle in the night air. There was a closeness between us as we talked, reinforced by the heavy darkness that surrounded us, making us feel isolated, alone in the world. Our voices echoed back to us, bouncing off the buildings and replaying the entire conversation after only a momentary lapse, giving our words an odd, surreal intangibility.

"Did you know that humans were once able to fly?" she asked me, her voice filled with amazement and curiosity but hushed as if calling from a million years ago. I just stared at her as we walked, unable to respond.

I stared up into the sky, a million stars peeking out from behind the black. "How many miles, can you imagine..." I stammered awkwardly. "How far away each little speck of light..."

Sedna had stopped walking and was staring directly into my face. "There is no millions of miles," she said soberly. "There is no 'out there'." She gazed upward, shaking her head. She reached up, grabbing with her hands at the stars.

"This is as big as my Universe is." she said then, stretching her arms to her sides and circling them around to illustrate the boundaries of her little world. "This is it; the Universe is really a lot smaller than people imagine."

After a moment, she added, "And a lot bigger than people imagine." She spoke slowly and quietly; words echoed off the rhythm of our steps. She turned her head toward me as she tried to explain. "If you think of the world on a subatomic level... even on an atomic level, where they've got everything charted out down to molecules; H2O, EtOH, and so on...

"If you think about the whole table of the elements, all hundred fourteen or something they've found now. Well, think of the table as an enormous novel, and each element is a chapter, so a hundred fourteen or whatever chapters...

"These letters we use to represent each one, H for hydrogen, N for nitrogen, these are only the first letters of each of the hundred fourteen chapters. You know how in old books, the first letter of a chapter is in an exaggerated, grotesque font? Well, this is kind of the same thought. That's all we see, the one letter, 'O means oxygen', but there's a couple thousand words that we don't even see, beyond each of those hundred fourteen letters. Do you kind of get it?"

I stared at her, unsure of how to interpret.

"Maybe," she said, reading my expression, "if you like my paintings enough, I will show you what I'm talking about." As we came to the strange-topped building, she stopped and regarded me with a toying glint in her eyes.

She led me inside and through a small security check, then down a long progression of grey, tepid hallways until at last we came to her door.

The room was bright, with faded orange walls. A strange cacophony of music confronted us as she opened the door. "My roommate is here," she said with a furrowing of her brow.

The room was incredibly cramped. The walls and roof seemed like little more than a skin that retracted and stretched with our movement. It was like standing inside a sickly sagging pumpkin, and the dull orange paint only reinforced the notion.

Two beds barely fit into the room. On the bed farther from the door sat the roommate, watching TV; I was shocked to realize she wasn't wearing clown makeup, but really looked like that.

Sedna didn't introduce us, and the roommate barely glanced up, engrossed as she was in some television program. She laughed loud and often, a fake-sounding, forced guffaw.

Sedna produced a large manila portfolio and laid it down on her bed. She untied the string holding it shut, and it bulged apart like a slow-dying accordion. The first painting she showed me was of a horse, trotting across a plain-looking field, against a plain-looking sky. It was well-executed, and she showed good technical skill as a painter, but the composition seemed to lack any imagination. The next painting was a lighthouse. A dog and some puppies.

"They're very well-done," I said, flipping through the canvases. I was looking at one of some dolphins. And in a fade of blue on the underside of one of the dolphins' fins, I saw what seemed to be a '6' under the paint.

I scanned around the painting, looking especially at the lighter colors, and could make out the little numbers underneath. I flipped back to the first painting, the horse in the field. And there in the light blue sky, just under the perfect yellow sun, hung a little '2', hidden behind some clouds.

I looked at Sedna. She was smiling at me expectantly. I felt somehow that I shouldn't mention I could tell they were color-by-numbers. I smiled and handed the stack of paintings back to her. "They're very well-done. You have good technical skill," I said.

She smiled shyly and tucked the paintings back into the portfolio. "Okay," she whispered, "I suppose you want to fly now."

We backed out of the tiny room into the hallway. I could still hear the roommate cackling away at the television. Sedna opened a door with a card key, and we entered the dark laboratory.

"The idea really came from studying changes in human anatomy over the last several thousand years," she explained as she moved about the room, turning on lights and computers and unfamiliar equipment. "Really simple things like the epidemics of varicose veins, bad knees and chronic back pain in humans in general point to the theory that maybe our body isn't meant to be used how it is currently used."

She strapped a harness around my torso; it was fitted with hundreds, maybe thousands, of little tabs that looked very much like electrodes but with a little light, possibly a laser, pointing out of each one. She then put on similar gloves, shoes and headgear. "Then studies were done on human anatomy to find what condition would be its ideal environment, and the almost unanimous result was: weightlessness."

She turned a dial on one of the unidentifiable devices, and all the tiny points of light attached to me lit up brilliant. I nearly lost my balance, stumbling back a step.

Sedna giggled and said, "Go ahead," nodding upward.

We were inside a giant dome, like an auditorium, but this was built to fly in. With almost no effort, just the thought of flight and an urge to rise, I felt myself lift off the ground.

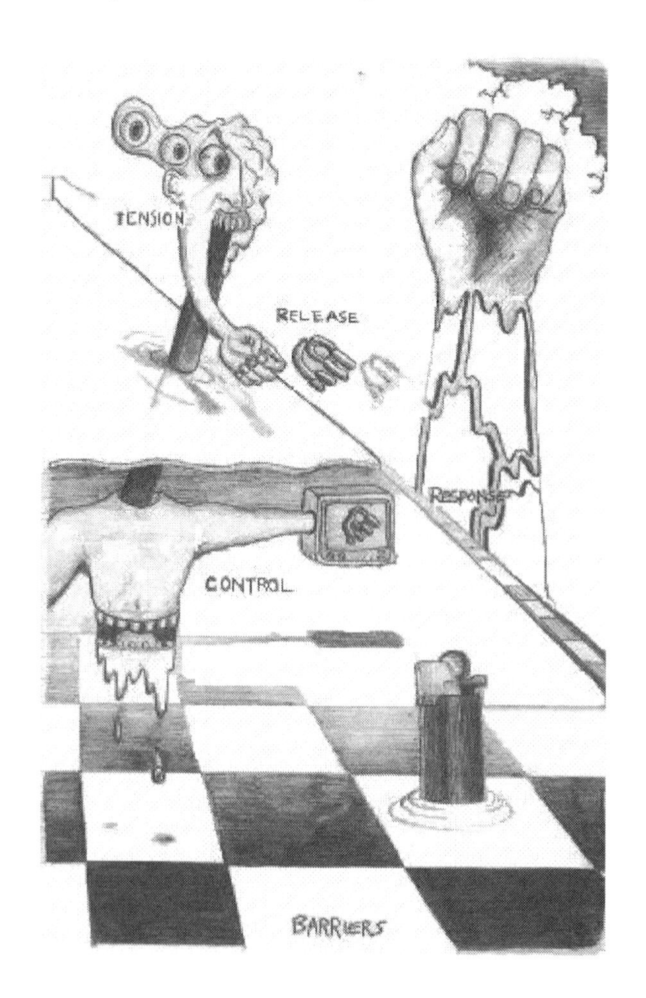

FLY

On a bus headed for the Appalachian Mountains, I found my life in danger thanks to the man seated next to me. He was wearing one of those illegal Explosion Suits, and by the look in his eyes, I knew it was due to go off at any moment.

I cleared my throat and turned toward him. "That's a mighty fine suit you have on there."

"Thanks," he said, sincere but obviously nervous. "It's made by Bigsby, Kruthers, Smith and Wesson. Cost me a bundle."

"I can imagine."

He was a stocky man, tanned and worn. Black, wavy hair dissipated on the top of his head, fading to a tarnished shade of silver. His eyes were kind, but the lines surrounding them scrunched and muddled into a map of one man's broken life. Somehow it had come to this, traveling through the country by bus, wearing an Explosion Suit.

"I bet when it goes off, though, it's quite a blast! Must be some sight to see!" I limply attempted conversation, hoping to seem as enthusiastic as I was terrified.

His eyes dropped to his shoes, and he mumbled a few syllables of acknowledgment and agreement.

An uneasy silence sat between us for a few moments before I gathered the courage to ask, "How often does it go off?"

BLAM!!! I must have uttered the trigger phrase; my dumb luck, always saying the wrong thing.

The whole bus exploded, and I found myself hurtling through the air, high above the Earth, my arms and legs flailing and grasping frantically for something, anything to hang on to.

I was reminded then of my third grade classroom, where I was asked once what I wanted to do when I grew up, and I said, "Fly."

My teacher, Mrs. Williams, was the first woman I ever had a crush on – the way her cheeks would blush up a rose color and her full lips would curl when I came to class late without my homework, or her tricky reprimanding gaze that hinted at silent approval when she caught me on the playground burning down the monkey bars.

"People cannot fly," she had said, the rest of the class laughing wildly around me. Her eyes had burned right into my skin, intimidating. My hands were bloated with sticky sweat, my forehead quickly overheating my body. "People cannot fly!"

Oh, Mrs. Williams, if you could only see me now, a couple thousand feet above the east coast, swirling around, twisting in the clouds and probably about to die. I hope there's something soft down there to land on...

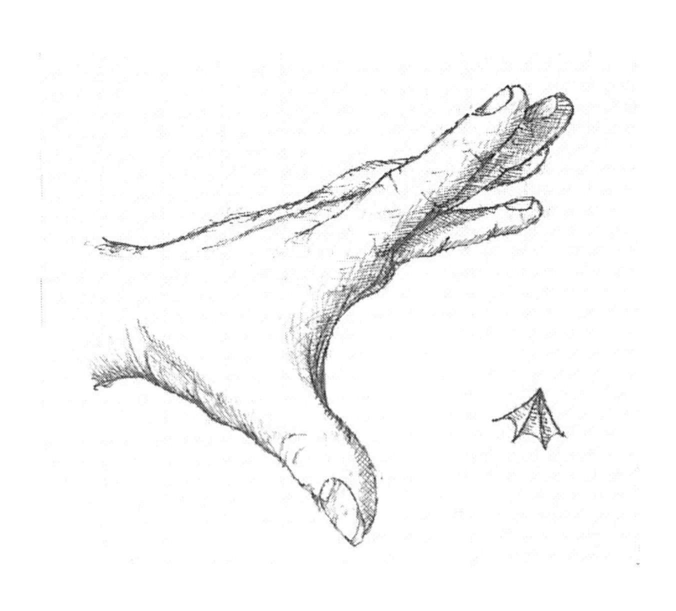

(invisibility)

About the Author

I
am a
pledge
drive on
PBS without
any guests to
go to and no one
behind me at the phones.

I,
the
guy who
can't give a
hot dog away
in Times Square at
rush hour on the day
after the last day of Lent.

Goo
goo
ga joob.

Apparently, my parents met before I was born. Many odd occurrences ensued.

At the age of two I was, for some reason, given a crayon. Within two weeks I had learned the alphabet.

In two more weeks I was eager to tackle my first novel. Unfortunately, I was very poor and could not afford paper until 1995, some twenty-three years later.

In those years I was restricted to drawing and writing on my clothes, around electrical sockets, and upon sugar packets. I held on to that first crayon until I was fifteen and finally able to beat up little kids for chalk.

I built my first guitar, a one-string self-electrocuting menacing placenta of ill-thought technology that never had a chance of being near tune, out of a Stradivarius I borrowed from a museum and bits of old smoke alarms.

More will be revealed as it becomes apparent...

Afterthought

This book is a very long time in the making. The earliest works contained here go back well over twenty years. There is an ever-expanding list of people I am grateful for and indebted to for their assistance or inspiration in bringing these stories to life.

First and foremost I have to thank my family, my mom, my sister and brothers, my nieces (!), my dad, all the extended relations branched out all over the world. Mark and Adam, the two friends I've had so long they might as well be family.

I especially want to express my thanks to the folks who helped with the construction of this collection, who made my work presentable and safe for humans: Katie, Kat, PT, Ted, Sandra, Tessa, Sherry, Randall, Tatyana, Lyndi, Amanda, Colleen, Elaina, Erin, Elizabeth, Adam, Jackson, Mary, Lem, Mariann, Haven, Diana, Terri-Ann, Kath, Stella, Duncan, EJ, Jennifer, Ash, Joyce, Tony, Dave, Christy, Pamela, Xyris and Dixie.

I attempted an all-inclusive list of the people I would like to thank, and it quickly proved longer than the actual text of this book, and I knew there were a ton of people I would miss. So excuse me for keeping this extremely brief, and forgive me if I have failed to mention you. Remind me, and I promise I'll put you in the next one (careful what you wish for...).

I want to thank everyone who inspired or assisted with these stories and everyone who has helped hone my craft.

I do want to thank everyone in Writer's World and Writer's Chest, everyone at Eat, Sleep, Write and Postcards, Poems and Prose, A Play on Words, Tough Critiques, and even that old Nano gaggle, even the ex-pats. You know who you are.

And, of course, you, the reader. I thank everyone who has spent time with my words and made the effort to read. I pray you found it fun and funny, and worthy of your time. My aim was to entertain and possibly enlighten or inspire.

Thank you for inviting me into your home. My final wish is that you have enjoyed visiting my world, and I do hope we meet again.

Robert Emmett
Dec 28, 2013
Outside Chicago, Inside my house,
Earth

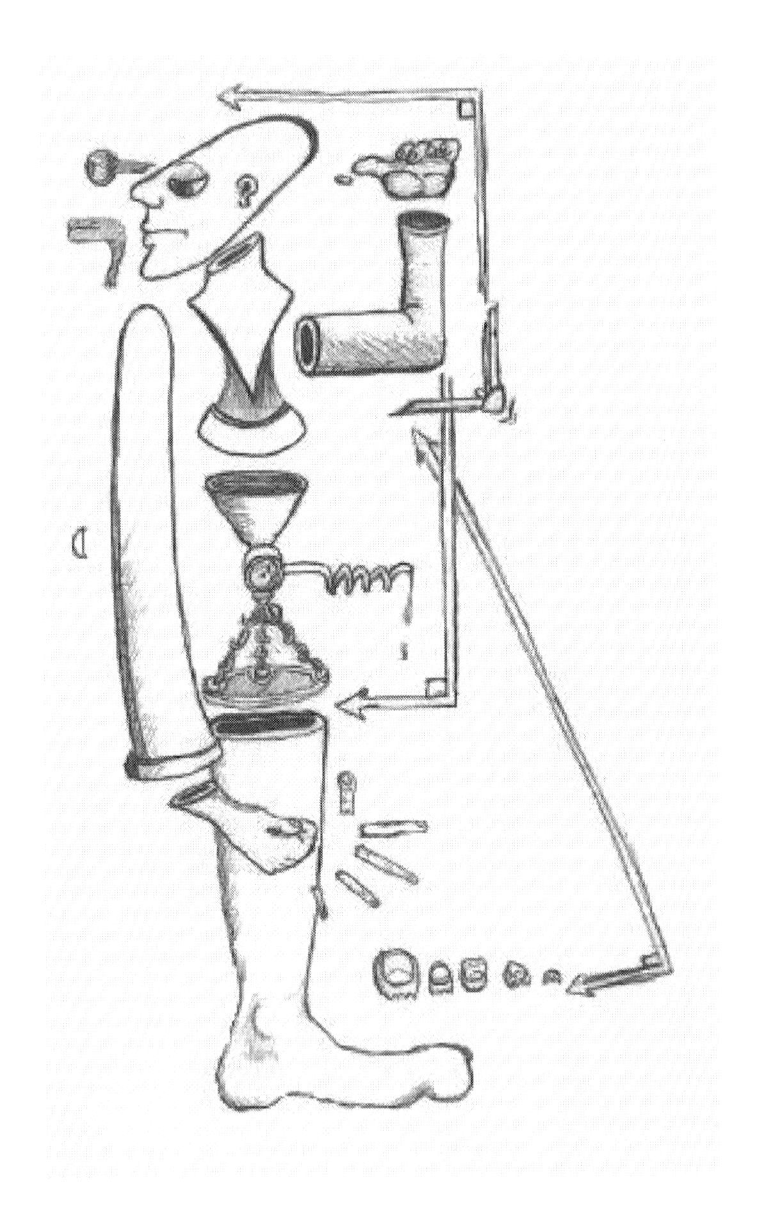

Made in the USA
Columbia, SC
10 February 2023

12150687R10100